About the author:

Oswald Pereira has worked in senior editorial positions for leading newspapers and magazines like *The Times of India, Financial Express* and *Outloo*k. He has taught journalism at *The Times School of Journalism*, and is also an English language trainer. He is a contributor to *The Speaking Tree* column in *The Times of India* and his spiritual articles have appeared in four *Speaking Tree* anthologies. Oswald was born in Thane, Maharashtra, and studied at St Xavier's College, Mumbai. He now lives with his wife and son in Noida.

CHADDI BUDDIES

Oswald Pereira

Srishti
PUBLISHERS & DISTRIBUTORS

SRISHTI PUBLISHERS & DISTRIBUTORS
Registered Office: N-16, C.R. Park
New Delhi – 110 019
Corporate Office: 212A, Peacock Lane
Shahpur Jat, New Delhi – 110 049
editorial@srishtipublishers.com

First published by
Srishti Publishers & Distributors in 2015

*To love,
friendship
and brotherhood.*

Acknowledgements

There is one person whom I cannot thank enough. She is my wife Reena Singh, who saw the manuscript with a fine toothcomb before I sent it out for publishing. An editor herself, she's always been the first person to read my manuscripts, give her incisive comments and suggest changes that always seem right.

However, my inspiration has always been my son Arjun. He never allows me to give up and when I am down and say, "Enough of writing," he comes up with the most encouraging and inspiring words: "Dad you are the world's best author".

I would like to thank team Srishti Publishers for their great warmth and invaluable suggestions on *Chaddi Buddies*. Their feedback and suggestions did wonders for the novel, making it a crisper and more engaging read.

A big thank you to Raymond Anto for his brilliant cover design.

A special thanks to my friend and senior journalist Ranjeni A Singh for suggesting an out-of-the-box title for the book.

I greatly cherish the memories of my late father Cyprian Pereira and my late mother Maisie Pereira. No words can thank them. My father had detected the writer in me when I was barely out of my teens and presented me with a Remington Rand typewriter to facilitate my writing.

He also gifted me the leather-bound Literary Heritage Collection of the great classics that cost a princely sum of Rs 21 each in those days. The collection was topped with four volumes of Shakespeare. However, I inherited my storytelling skills from my mother, who used to regale us seven siblings for hours with her stories that she narrated complete with sounds and acting.

We seven siblings created a great ruckus at home, competing with each other in shouting over the din, in order to be heard. Festivals were celebrated with song and dance to the accompaniment of the guitar. After marriage, we lived in different cities and abroad, but almost every Christmas, we have got together for a family reunion and to relive the old fun times, singing and making merry. So, the last but most important string of thanks goes out to my siblings – Collin, Elphege, Cora, Marlene, Juliet and Lenny.

The good times that we had together have been a great inspiration for *Chaddi Buddies.*

Prologue

Hill Mansion was a house that I used to visit stealthily, because my parents would have grounded me if they learnt that I socialised with the residents there. On a few occasions when my brothers discovered my secret visits, I had to bribe them with my week's pocket money to keep mum.

Going by its glorious name and majestic location – atop a small hill on the outskirts of our village Golvada, overlooking lush woods where birds cooed while mating and a couple of peacocks strutted around – Hill Mansion should have been a subject of envy. Instead, it was an object of ridicule. But to me, it was the best address in our village.

My home, 'White House' was among the first modern, concrete-and-cement structures with a proper terrace to come up in Golvada that had mud and brick structures for houses with red, conical Mangalore-tiled roofs. Yet I believed Hill Mansion was far superior to White House because I chose that name. And my best friends Anand and Baloo – and their elder brother Dattya, my hero – lived there.

So what if Hill Mansion was no mansion but a ramshackle hut with a tin roof that rattled with the smallest gust of wind!

One day when I arrived at Anand and Baloo's home with a tin board reading 'Hill Mansion', painted in red by me from the leftover paint at my home, the two looked puzzled. They were not baffled with the name because they couldn't read; they were illiterate.

When I explained the meaning of Hill Mansion to them, their perplexed faces lit up. They got to work, propping up the board in front of their hut on two bamboo poles stuck into the ground. When the job was done, they hugged me.

I could smell their sweat because they bathed only once a week owing to water shortage. They had to trek down a kilometer from Hill Mansion for their supply of water from the village public tap. Since they were not bona fide residents of the village, their home being an illegal structure, their turn to fill water came last – and often, by the time they reached the tap, it was past water hours. The two buckets of water that Anand and Baloo sometimes managed to fetch was not enough to cook, do the dishes and bathe for the six residents of Hill Mansion. The three brothers lived there with their parents and sister, Shalu, a year younger than Dattya.

Hill Mansion – a hut barely fifteen by ten feet – was sometimes knocked down by storms and rains and rebuilt by the family each time. Anand and Baloo made sure that the board was always on display. I never visited Hill Mansion at night, because it was too dark and wild foxes roamed freely, but Anand and Baloo said they hung a small kerosene lamp above the board that glowed at night. That was in the late fifties, when I was a little more than nine years old.

The only way to
Heaven is through Christ!

Friday, the 4th of November, 1960, is a day that I'll never forget. It was the day when Father Francis Fonseca, a jovial, portly priest, with a long white beard like Santa Claus announced the good news to us in catechism class. The good news was from the messiah Lord Jesus Christ, and His messenger Father Francis Fonseca made the announcement with great joy in his voice, his eyes beaming with a strange, bright light.

"The only way to heaven is through Christ," Father Francis, my favourite priest, whom I adored like he were God himself, declared. I was Father Francis' favourite because in catechism class, I would score anything from 97 to 100 marks, the highest in religion. The books that I received for the highest marks at annual award functions were proudly displayed in our showcase at home. My mother Mavis Pereira made sure that the books were always in the front row of the showcase, whose glass front she dusted with great care.

She was both happy and sad that I scored such high marks in religion – happy that I was so bright and good in religion, but sad that the marks were not counted in the general total while allotting ranks to students. Religion class was an extracurricular activity, like sports, where even if you were the best, it wasn't ever added to your scholastic scores. My mother was happy that my high scores in religion meant that I loved God, but she was sad that I would become so holy that when I grew up, I might join the priesthood. She loved me too much and didn't want to lose me to the priesthood.

But like my mother's mixed feelings of happiness and sadness about my marks, I too was both happy and sad at Father Francis' announcement of a heaven through Christ for good practising Catholics.

I was only ten years old and heaven seemed so many years away for me. But the thought that it was a privilege that I would enjoy because I was a Catholic made me feel like dancing with joy. But then after the initial euphoria of the good tidings, an overwhelming sadness descended on me and tears trickled down my eyes.

Father Francis was not an emotional sort and didn't like people shedding tears for no rhyme or reason. He wanted all of us to be strong. So, he didn't like me crying one bit, especially when I should have been clapping my hands in appreciation of the good news. But since I was his favourite, he came very close to me and put his hands on my shoulders most tenderly. I had no clue about how a saint smelled. But many of my classmates had awful breath because I think they didn't brush their teeth regularly. Father Francis' breath on me was so fresh and pure that for a while, I felt he was not a human being, but some sort of a saint. And the otherwise strict priest had such a kind smile on his face that it reminded me of the pictures that I had seen of various saints and of the Lord Jesus Himself.

"Why are you crying, Robert?" Father Francis asked, in a tender voice.

I didn't reply, but started crying more, just short of wailing.

"Why are you crying, Robert? Tell me," Father Francis asked again, coming closer than before, that saintly breath now hitting my face like a knife.

Yes, like a knife. How could I tell my saintly, God-like Father Francis that his good news, that, at first, seemed a reason to celebrate, was now a cause for mourning and sorrow?

Realising that I was inconsolable, Father Francis went back to his chair and continued his homily on how we were lucky to be born Christians, or more specifically Catholics, because there was Heaven waiting for us, of course, only if we were good boys and girls and loved God with our whole heart and soul.

I heard him in a daze, averting my eyes each time he looked at me.

When there were ten minutes left for the class to end, Father Francis as usual stopped talking and invited us to ask questions. I always asked more than half the questions.

This time around, I had only one question, but I didn't ask it, because I was afraid that the answer would make me wail and the rest of the class, laugh.

As Father Francis finished his class, he came up to me sitting in the first row, and patted me on my shoulder. I looked up at him without tears in my eyes, because they had dried up by then.

When I reached home looking sad, my mother, who was preparing the meal for our family of five children, almost jumped from her seat in the kitchen.

"What happened, Robert? Did someone tease you in school?" she asked, hugging me.

For a moment, I was tempted to ask her the question that I hadn't asked Father Francis, but then I quickly changed my mind, because I knew she too would be of little help in the matter.

That left me with only one choice. To ask the question, whose answer I was afraid to hear, to God Himself. But it was a question that I couldn't ask in front of the whole household, because you hardly get privacy to talk to God in such a large family.

So at midnight, when everyone was asleep, I knelt in front of the altar in the living room and bowed my head reverentially.

When I had mustered enough courage, I looked up and whispered the question to Lord Jesus hanging from a miniature cross, looking so kind and compassionate, "Dear Jesus, if the only way to heaven is through you, what happens to my friends Anand and Baloo, and Dattya Dada who are Hindus and don't believe in you?"

I wasn't expecting an answer, but I was relieved of the pain and sorrow I felt at the catechism class, because I, for some childish reason believed that He would welcome Anand and Baloo into heaven because they were my friends – and, of course their elder brother Dattya too would be there because he was my hero.

The last man

I scored the highest marks in religion, but made the lowest runs in our Golvada village cricket team. In matches with nearby villages, I never got a chance to play in the team because there were so many better cricketers than me. Our team rarely lost a match and prided in calling itself Gold Winners Club. I was not even taken as an extra in the team. An extra could chip in as a runner when a batsman got injured.

But I couldn't run fast enough to be included in the team. I was too slow and clumsy to be a runner. That earned me the nickname 'Pondya' in Marathi, which means an indolent, feeble fellow, too lazy to exert himself.

I was also called 'Bhomya' at home, the equivalent of 'Pondya' in the Marathi East Indian dialect, my father and grandmother's mother tongue that my Anglo-Indian mother spoke well too, though we kids preferred to speak in English. My grandmother kept assuring me that Bhomya sounded better than Pondya. I was naturally not happy with my two nicknames.

My physical status as a boy was a legacy of my baby days when I was overweight and slept during a large part of the day and night. I never kept my parents awake, bawling like other babies, I was told. My mother was a happy person at night, but she was a worried woman during the day. Grandma told me later when I grew up that my mother's pretty, fair forehead crinkled when she saw me lying on the baby cot, more chubby than other kids, and with a ravenous appetite for milk. Mother's worries multiplied as I grew in months.

While other babies took their first steps when they were barely ten months old, I continued to crawl even at fourteen months. My body was too heavy to stand and walk. No matter how much my parents tried to make me stand and walk, I couldn't, because of my bulk. Grandmother told me how my mother would sometimes break down and weep, while I just looked up at her, smiling, the dimple in my fat right cheek looking cute.

But my cuteness was marred with my rather strange habit of neighing like a baby horse, which disturbed my mother no end. My grandmother, though, loved my neighing. Her theory was that the neighing was a good sign as it meant that I would be a winning horse in life. She kept consoling my mother about my bulkiness and the futuristic aspect of my neighing, but that didn't provide the trigger for me to walk.

I don't recall this incident at all. But grandma described how one fine day, while my mother was busy cooking in the kitchen, I neighed louder than ever, stood up, held the front of the showcase in the living room and took my first steps.

Grandmother was enjoying herself on the rocking chair and was too stunned to even cry with joy. She didn't even call out to my mother because she was not sure if she had really seen me walk and suspected that she might have been dreaming. I continued crawling for some time. Then I neighed again, very loud, attracting the attention of my mother who came running to the living room and screamed with joy when she saw me walking, though rather unsteadily because of my bulky baby body.

By the time I reached school-going age, I had lost all my baby fat and was transformed into a thin, skinny kid. But the clumsiness seemed to have stayed in my bones. I was not knock-kneed or flat-footed, but I couldn't run fast. Given that I was taller than most boys of my age, my long legs should have been an asset. Why they weren't so, God only knew. I was not as strong as the other kids. But why? I didn't know the answer.

All said and done, God was not unkind to me. He gave me a nice smiling face and a sharp mind. And to fend off the wicked and cruel, I was gifted with a loud voice and a fiery temper that I hoped would scare away my adversaries. The neighing of a baby was upgraded by the Almighty into the growl of a lion cub. But I doubt if anyone was afraid of this.

My siblings at home found my growl irritating, but my best friends Anand and Baloo's elder brother Dattya loved it. Dattya was my hero, because he was the captain of our cricket team, the best pace bowler, and the highest run scorer.

The fact that he was the son of 'Gangu Bai', who washed and cleaned people's dishes and homes in our village didn't go against his captaincy. Dattya always emerged as the man of the match, and he led our village's team to victory not only by his great captaincy, but also by his superb performance in every match.

I looked up to Dattya because he was the only person who appreciated my talent in confusing the best of players by my loud and growling appeals of 'How's that?' without any reason. My appeals didn't get a person out, but it shattered the confidence and concentration of the best of players, including my elder brother Victor who could stick to the crease like a leech, just playing steady, hardly scoring any runs. Sometimes he would go as opening batsman and barely score any runs. But he was a pillar of strength that we needed to exhaust the opponent.

When we played friendly cricket matches among ourselves in the village, Dattya always included me in his team. I was put in the front in fielding and kept shouting, "How's that, umpire?" I couldn't field and missed the easiest of catches, but that didn't matter to my hero Dattya.

But even Dattya couldn't include me in matches against other village teams, because my shouting ability would not compensate for my poor cricketing skills. I consoled myself that Dattya didn't include even his brothers Anand and Baloo in the cricket team, though they were better cricketers than me. But the reason for not including his brothers had nothing to do with cricketing. It was more for economic reasons.

There were no compulsory fees to join Gold Winners Club. But when it came to playing matches, those who didn't pay didn't qualify as players, because one needed good bats, stumps and balls to play. Dattya did odd jobs working at construction sites and as a casual labourer in factories. So he was more loaded with money than even some of the village boys, because our parents were not very liberal with pocket money in those days. So Dattya was in the team as captain because of his good cricket, leadership skills and his money.

Then one afternoon after school when I had sneaked up to Hill Mansion to meet Anand and Baloo, I learnt the secret of Dattya's prowess in cricket and his rippling muscles. As my friends and I strolled in the woods behind Hill Mansion, we saw Dattya exercise. I counted a hundred pushups in slow, steady, rhythmic movements and double the amount of baithaks or squats. Tufts of hair fell over his sweaty forehead, which Dattya wiped with the back of his hand. He had an oval-shaped, dark brown handsome face, with a firm chin and snow white teeth that came from brushing with the twig of a neem tree.

He grinned as he rose from the ground and waved out to me, saying, "Hello Samson". Apart from Anand and Baloo, Dattya was the third person in Golvada among the younger lot who called me 'Samson', while the rest loved the sound of the word 'Pondya'.

As Dattya took a three-minute break, he urged me to try my hand at it. I did three pushups and collapsed on the mud. The three brothers cheered and patted me on my back, so vigorously and warmly that it warmed my sad heart.

After his exercise, Dattya sat on a stool in the backyard of Hill Mansion and I discovered more about the secret of his strength. That secret was his afternoon meal. It consisted of six big bajra rotis, two onions and three long green chilies. I have never seen till this day, anyone enjoy a meal the way Dattya did. He slurped at each bite and licked his fingers, making varying sounds of satisfaction that I find difficult to describe here.

After Dattya finished his meal, he told us what he called a top secret. I was being included as the last man in the batting order in the next match. But he had one condition to the offer.

It was one helluva condition.

I had to eat a bajra roti, with a small onion and a thin long chili. Anand and Baloo protested vehemently at the condition and called their Dada mean and wicked. But Dattya didn't relent. I accepted reluctantly.

I didn't enjoy a single bite of the bajra roti, though the onion, which Dattya broke for me with his strong fist, tasted like roasted chicken in comparison. The chilli burnt my tongue no end. Dattya kept goading me on, "Come on Samson, buck up Samson," while Anand and Baloo patted me on my back as I swallowed, my eyes half-closed, my face, a painful grimace. I downed three long aluminum tumblers of water, which was a precious commodity in Hill Mansion. But when my meal was over, there was a huge round of applause from the three brothers.

That, however, was only the first round of training in my initiation into Gold Winners Club as the last man. We went out into the woods and choosing a flat ground deep inside, Dattya bowled his dangerous pace balls. Luckily, we played village cricket with tennis balls in those days. So serious injury was ruled out. We used stones for stumps, because Dattya didn't keep the cricket equipment of the team with him for fear it may be stolen from their hut.

I was clean bowled by Dattya a number of times. Then he would come up to me and explain how I should have fended the ball and hit it across. After failing to connect a single ball in one hour, I finally managed to nick one delivery. The next delivery was faster and threatened to hit me in the face, but I stepped back at the last moment and hit it hard over Dattya's head. He jumped high up into the air and held the ball neatly with both hands and yelled, "How's that, umpire?"

"Out," I said, as I flung the bat on the ground and started weeping.

Dattya came up to me and held me tenderly. Anand and Baloo, who were the fielders, ran up to me and hugged me too. The brothers took turns to wipe off my tears.

Dattya gave me a gentle smack on my cheek and said, "Samson, come play again." But he showed no mercy in his bowling and pitched a number of fast deliveries, all of which I failed to touch.

Dattya had been bowling for more than an hour with very short breaks but his pitch and pace never faltered. Then he bowled his most gigantic delivery of the afternoon. I hit back the ball with all my might. The ball went well over Dattya's head deep into the woods. While Anand and Baloo went scampering into the wild trees to look for the ball, Dattya ran up to me and gave me a mighty bear hug.

The gruelling batting practice sessions with me continued for a month, one hour a day. I learnt all manner of strokes – hitting the ball on the back foot, stepping in front and smashing the ball, sweeping the ball, and punishing a careless full-toss. Dattya was a strict task master, but with a touch of kindness.

After the end of my training, satisfied that I was good enough, he announced, "Congratulations, Samson, you are inshide team az lasht man."

My first match

Sunday, the 4th of June, 1961 was one of the happiest days in the life of the ten years and nine months old Robert Pereira – that's yours truly.

It was a pleasant and bright morning. The Gold Winners Club team led by the tall, dark and handsome captain, Dattaram 'Dattya' Bhoir, aged fifteen, marched towards Tembi Naka, to take on our opponents, the Tembi Tandavas, with whom we had lost a match once, but won the rest of the three played with them so far. I was panting as I tried to keep pace with Dattya. After a while, he deliberately slowed down so that I could walk in tandem with him.

The previous evening, when we had assembled at the village cross, our favourite meeting place in the centre of the village, and Dattya had announced my inclusion in the team, at least two core team members threatened to walk out of the match in protest. They were my thirteen-year-old elder brother Victor and my classmate, Clarence D'Silva, the vice-captain, who was a great spin bowler and hard hitter. Dattya had emitted a very loud, *phoot* – get lost – at their protests. He clenched both his fists into two neat but dangerous looking balls, threatening to aim it at their faces as they mockingly asked, "What, are you mad that you are allowing Pondya to play in our team?"

Dattya held both Victor and Clarence in his strong arms, squeezed their necks, and warned in Marathi, "This is the last time you are calling my younger brother Pondya."

Now as we continued our march towards Tembi Naka, Victor and Clarence overtook Dattya and me with rapid strides. My friends Anand and Baloo jumped into the fray on my behalf. They had been walking a few paces behind Dattya and me, but now they galloped ahead. In a moment, they had raced Clarence and Victor, increasing their pace to the speed of trotting ponies.

At twelve, Anand was tall, almost the height of Dattya. He was quite bulky too. While Dattya's long hair was dark brown and combed flat, Anand's hair was curly and black, like his dark complexion, earning for him the nickname, Kaliya. Baloo was a couple of inches shorter than me, and was my age.

A bit plumpish, Baloo's face was full of pockmarks. But his forever smiling face hid the blemish. Golvada boys had nicknamed him *Badh* (drought), because they cruelly joked that his face resembled a dried up field that develops deep cracks without water.

As Anand and Baloo kept turning around, whistling and booing Victor and Clarence, I heard Victor tell Clarence, "Let's not try and race those '*junglees*.' I want to preserve my energy to score a century."

But Victor, the opening batsman was out for a duck in the first ball of the match.

Dattya had won the toss and decided to field, because he preferred the strategy of chasing a total and knocking the opponent off for a small total, when his bowlers and fielders were fresh. The strategy worked as the Tembi Tandavas were bundled out for fifty runs. Dattya captured five of the ten wickets with his deadly bowling. Clarence with his deceptive spin got three wickets and Ashley D'Mello and Imran Ali took one wicket each.

Before going to bat, Victor had bragged that he would score the fifty runs alone by himself.

Now that he was out, he crept up to me and whispered in my right ear, "Panvati Pondya", a double insult to me, because to my nickname was added the tag, 'the one who brings bad luck,' which was how we all understood the word 'Panvati'. Not only as captain, but even otherwise, Dattya's ears were always pricked up, even in sleep, as he had to be alert to the foxes that sometimes attacked their lonely home. He had not only chased but even killed a couple of foxes in the dead of the night with a club that he kept near him when he slept. Dattya apparently heard Victor's double insult to me. He turned red with anger, but controlled himself because he couldn't lose his temper as captain.

Instead, he came up to me and ruffled my hair, saying, "Samson, me iz coming tenth man and I iz batting with you." I don't know why he said this, because fifty runs was easy to score for us, despite the fall of Victor's wicket. He was needed at number five, his usual batting order, to speed up the run rate. In past matches, when other batsmen collapsed, Dattya would stand like a bulldozer, ripping off runs from every bowler.

After Victor's wicket, Neville, our most stylish player, came in to bat at his usual number three position. After a few stylish strokes that didn't have much power, he hit the fifth ball of the match for two runs. He then nicked the last ball of the first over with too much movement of his bat but not enough concentration with the result that it slipped into the hands of the alert wicket keeper, who took an easy catch.

We were now two wickets down for two runs in the first over of the match. Sensing danger, Dattya promoted Clarence, the hitter, from number six to number four in the batting order, to break Tembi Tandava's wicket-taking spree. Clarence and Imran, the other batsman, seemed to be the right combination. Since Imran was a single run specialist, he always gave the other batsman the chance to score the big runs.

Now Imran patted a ball away and ran almost with it, while Clarence sprinted across to complete a single. Clarence then smashed two balls in quick succession to the boundary line.

He hit the next ball hard, but it didn't connect well enough, with the result that the bowler himself gingerly stepped a few paces ahead and took a nice catch.

Eleven runs for three wickets didn't seem like a comfortable score at all. So, all eyes turned to Dattya, who went at number five. My hero, captain Dattya smiled benignly at his dejected team players. I didn't smile as I was nervous and felt guilty, believing that I was really the 'panvati' that had brought bad luck to our team. Then Dattya surprised everyone when he asked Suresh Mahadik, fourth in the batting order, who had been superseded by Clarence to go at Dattya's number five position.

The strike now went to Imran, who scored a single in the very first ball of the next over, the strike going to Suresh. But Suresh was out in the next ball without scoring! Four wickets down for twelve runs was a poor show.

Dattya didn't go in at number six either, which he should have done to stall the collapse, and instead let the batting order stay with the usual sixth man Vinayak Deshpande being sent in to bat. I was praying that Vinayak would score. I also wanted him to shine because he was the only boy who supported my entry into the team for this match.

As I closed my eyes in prayer, asking God to help us in this game because it was my first match, I was jolted by a loud roar – the pavilion seemed to have gone berserk.

Vinayak had hit the ball for a six. Our score had climbed up to eighteen. Vinayak then quietened down and played the other balls of the over with a slow, steady bat.

Then the whole pavilion including captain Dattya uttered a collective sigh of disappointment when Imran's middle stump was knocked off by the second ball of the next over that came straight and fast, taking him completely by surprise.

Five wickets down for eighteen runs was clearly a collapse.

I expected Dattya would now go in to bat, despite him telling me he would be tenth man. But he didn't budge, prompting Victor and Clarence to troop up to him. "Dattya go and bat now, enough of your drama," Victor demanded.

Dattya merely smiled and said, "Ralph going now. I iz going az tenth man."

"Why?" Victor asked loudly, shooting daggers at me.

"To play with my hero Samson," he said.

"You are a *veda,* a mad man," Victor said.

Clarence was more diplomatic and said, "Dattya please save Gold Winners Club."

"Don't you worries, we two iz going to save," Dattya said, holding me by the shoulder.

Clarence opened his mouth to utter an expletive. I could see it form in his mouth. But as Dattya took his hand off my shoulder and puffed up his chest, the veins in his muscular neck thickening, Clarence swallowed the expletive without uttering it. So Ralph, the tallest member of our team, went in at number seven.

Ralph, a hit out and get out batsman, hit the first ball that he played for a four, pushing our total to twenty-two. There was some jubilation in the pavilion, but it soon died down as we waited for Ralph to face the next ball. Like a daredevil, Ralph, whom we fondly called Polly Umrigar because of his playing style, ran in front of the crease when the ball was bowled with the intention of lifting it for a six. But Ralph missed the ball completely and turned to run back to his crease.

However, he was too late, for the wicket keeper smartly knocked off all the stumps, making Ralph our sixth casualty.

Eighth in the batting order was the lean but strong thirteen-year-old Milton Aguiar. Though not a top scorer, Milton sometimes scored a few quick useful runs in matches.

But Milton was valued the most for his generosity, as he always ensured the club had a regular supply of balls. His family ran a transport business and he was never short of cash. However, Milton never lost an opportunity to poke fun at me and always addressed me as Pondya, unlike the others who still occasionally call me by my real name, Robert. Whenever Milton looked at me, it was with a smug, taunting expression on his face. As he went in to bat, he stopped near me, wearing that same expression.

But his smugness seemed to have paid off as he smashed the fifth ball of the over for a four through a gap between the fielders, taking our total to twenty-six runs. However, when Milton had a go at the last ball of the over, he missed it completely, with the result that his off stump was knocked down. We were now seven wickets down.

Then Dattya sent Ashley in at number nine. He was no batsman and luckily for him, since Milton was out on the last ball, he didn't have to take strike. It was Vinayak who had to bat.

Vinayak played the first ball silently. Then he got adventurous in the second ball and had a wild go at it. His bat connected. But he had played cross bat, with the result that the ball didn't move far and instead went high up in the air. The first slip, a short, thin boy sprinted towards the ball, almost missed it, but dived for it in the nick of time and held it up, clear off the ground, though he had fallen down.

Gold Winners Club was eight wickets down for twenty-six runs, needing twenty-five runs to win. The captain who had demoted himself to number ten for my sake, walked in to bat, coolly, grinning without sign of panic.

But I was disappointed, for Dattya played all the remaining four balls of the over in a lacklustre manner, without scoring, and leaving the strike to Ashley in the next over. On the second ball, Ashley was declared out – leg before wicket.

There were still four more balls to go in the over, when I, the last man, started walking into the field to take strike in my first match.

There was an eerie, almost ghostly silence in the pavilion. Then as I neared the crease, I felt like the sky was going into a tailspin.

Dattya made a sign to the umpire, indicating that he wanted to speak to me. The umpire nodded his permission. The captain met me, shook hands with me firmly and said, "Samson we iz going to win." Then he walked back to the non-striker's end.

It all seemed like a blur then. But now as I write, the memory seems so vivid. I played my first ball with a bat that was shaking so much that I feared that it would fall off my hands. But luckily my bat touched the ball that crawled towards the first slip.

Oh! Why was I so nervous when Dattya had so nicely taught me to bat for a whole month? I felt that I had let down my captain. But when I looked up at him to see if he was angry, he had such a loving, encouraging smile on his face.

But even Dattya's love didn't make me brave enough to look at the bowler and his hand movement, which my captain had advised I should do, as this was very important to anticipate what the ball would be. I, nevertheless, succeeded in pushing the fourth ball of the over away from me with a straight bat. It struck me that the tremors in my hand had reduced.

When I played the fifth ball, I shook a little, but hit the ball a bit. The sixth ball came so rapidly that I missed it completely. It knocked down two of the three stumps along with the bails. But as I was walking away, really dejected that I had proven to be a loser, the umpire shook his head. Dattya too was smiling. I wondered why, because I was clean bowled.

Then Dattya shouted from across, "Samson, you not out. That waz no ball."

While I was happy that I had survived, the thought that I would have to face another last ball in the over was driving me crazy. The bowler now delivered a full toss, apparently to tempt me to hit so that he would get a nice catch. I was no hitter and quietly patted the ball down. And I wasn't trembling at all, as I achieved the feat of playing this ball too. I crossed over to the non-striker's end, feeling extremely relaxed.

Dattya played the first two balls quietly down towards the bowler, without any hurry in the world. The captain gave the same gentle treatment to the next three balls, all good deliveries, fast and accurate, which would have ripped off the stumps if Dattya hadn't played them well. Now it was the last ball of the over and I found myself beginning to tremble with the thought that if Dattya hit this ball for a four, it would put me at the striking end again.

My worst fears came true because Dattya hit the ball for not a four, but a six, raising the total to thirty-two, but leaving the strike to me in the upcoming over. I was scared to hell. I had to face the next six balls. It was the same bowler that I was to face. I noticed him smile.

The first two balls were full tosses. I patted them down. What a waste of full tosses. If Dattya had been given such deliveries, he would have lifted them for sixes. The third, fourth and fifth balls were full tosses, but I again played them down tamely. I looked up at the bowler. He was grinning. He might have thought I was an idiot. I avoided looking at Dattya, as I felt I had let him down. Then I thought of my grandmother's words, "A neighing child will turn out to be a winning horse."

The bowler walked back to take his short run-up to the wicket. I dared to look at his bowling arm. He was not going to bowl a full toss. He was probably planning to knock off my stumps and laugh at me. I neighed like a horse and stepped forward, jumping a few inches into the air. I converted the ball into a full toss by attacking it before it got me and lifted it up for a six. There was a deadpan silence in the pavilion; then a wild round of applause. I couldn't believe that I had done it, as I looked at my thin, spindly arms.

When I crossed the field to exchange strikes, Dattya stopped in the centre of the field. He had tears in his eyes. As I stood at the non-striker's end, it struck me that I might have broken a record in village cricket – the first last man to have opened his account with a six.

Gold Winners Club was thirty-eight runs for nine wickets. We still needed thirteen runs to win the game. I hoped Dattya would score these runs in the over that he was playing. For him, it was like child's play, because he had done it in many past matches. But Dattya didn't score a single run in the over and quietly played every ball, steadily.

When the same smiling, grinning bowler came out to bowl to me in the next over, he looked very serious. His first ball was straight and neat bang on the stumps. I didn't neigh this time, but went on the back foot and hit the ball as hard as I could. Dattya signalled that we take a run and I crossed over to the other side for an easy single.

Now it was the once-smiling-grinning-bowler-turned-serious-face who was bowling to our captain, who seemed to be laughing to himself. Dattya hit the second and third balls of the over for two consecutive fours. Now at forty-seven runs, we were just four short of victory. Dattya couldn't do much with the fourth and fifth balls. It was now the last ball of the over and I was praying hard that he would hit it for a four and score the winning stroke.

The bowler was grinning again as he delivered a full toss to Dattya, who hit it towards long on, but not hard enough for a boundary. We went for two runs, but couldn't take three, which would have put Dattya at the striking end.

When I crossed over to the field, I accosted my captain and asked him bluntly, "Why aren't you hitting, Dada?"

"Phoot Samson," he said, with a wicked smile on his face.

We needed two more runs to win, which would have been a cakewalk for Dattya. But for me it seemed like an impossible feat. As I played each of the five balls with a straight, steady bat, not scoring any runs but still holding on to my wicket, I would look up at Dattya. I could see his face plastered with that same wicked smile.

I had got the message. So when the last ball was bowled, I hit it so hard that I felt like my elbow had cracked, because it made a grating sound with the effort. But I was relieved to learn that the cracking sound came from a broken bat.

I was in a daze. The ball had gone across the boundary line for a four.

Our team in the pavilion was wild with joy. I found myself being lifted on the shoulders of my best friends Anand and Baloo. As they put me down on the ground, I saw Dattya holding out four tickets of Dev Anand's blockbuster movie, *CID*.

"I booking deeze in advhance for us to celebrate our win," he said and hugged me. We were both crying in each other's arms.

Anand and Baloo were jumping high up in the air, whistling and clapping.

Those were the days

In our village Golvada in Thana, we didn't know the difference between religion, caste, creed and class. In Golvada, Hindus, Muslim and Christian children played and laughed together. Our favourite meeting place during the day after school was an ancient banyan tree, which blessed us with its shade and was big enough to accommodate the whole gang of youngsters.

The only day when we didn't sit under the banyan tree was on the annual 'Wad Puja'. On puja day, elegant women, in their best finery would go around the banyan tree, wrapping it with thread, offering *aartis* to the sacred tree, praying that their husbands would have a long and healthy life like the strong and sturdy tree.

Behind the tree was a Shiva temple. When devotees rang its bells, it seemed like music to our ears. But we continued with our childish talk, even as worshippers walked in and out of the temple.

Barely thirty feet away from the banyan tree was the village well. Both children and adults swam in the village well. Labourers working in mills and factories, who were not residents of Golvada and lived in hutments some distance away, without access to a public tap or any other source of water, used to bathe at the well and carry home water in the same buckets that they used for bathing.

When Catholics in the village got married, a day before the wedding ceremony, water would be drawn from the well as it was an age-old custom called 'Umbracha Pani'. The bride-to-be and other women in the family would wear traditional pink saris. They would go dancing to the well to draw water. Relatives and friends danced along behind the bride with a pink umbrella.

The village well would be adorned with white strips of paint to mark the occasion. Before going to Church, the marriage party would also go to the Shiv Mandir to pay obeisance. The ancestors of Catholics in the village, my grandmother told me, were Hindus some centuries ago. So they retained a lot of Hindu customs.

But the fact that Hindus, Muslims and Christians were like brothers became more evident every evening, when boys of all faiths would meet at the cross in the centre of the village. We would sit on the steps of the cross. But unlike the banyan tree, the cross was not big enough to host the whole gang, so late comers had to stand.

Entertainment for us was Hindi movies in Prabhat Talkies, the only theatre in town. As pocket money was limited, we saw movies sitting on wooden benches on the first rows. The ticket was priced at five annas and later at fifty paise.

The movie that we were going to see was a treat from Dattya, who had spent two rupees on the four tickets. He had full faith that I would score the winning stroke. Based on that faith, he had risked the match and his credibility as captain, which he had won with so much of hard work.

I hoped that this one match would help in shedding a bit of the 'Pondya' tag that had haunted me for the past so many years. To me, Dattya was a saviour. I now loved and adored him as much as Jesus.

In the past too, Dattya had escorted me and other boys to many movies, like we were his younger brothers. He always paid for his own ticket and even treated us to a packet of wafers, which came in really tiny packs. Sometimes Anand and Baloo too would accompany us to the movies, after we had pooled in money for their tickets.

The only public transport within the city was the tonga, which as children we couldn't afford; so all our outings, including movies, were on foot.

All this friendship was, however, outside my home. My 'poor' friends Anand, Baloo and my hero and saviour Dattya, whom I called Dada, never visited me at home. They couldn't socialise with the family, because they were children of a 'servant'.

The class divides and religious differences stared me in the face at home. Anand, Baloo and Dattya could never join in our Christian festivals or enjoy celebrations in the village like weddings, which was a full week of merry making in those days.

We never sent them a Christmas cake.

I found this so unfair and sad.

It gave me sleepless nights. I would cry silently with my head buried in my pillow when I thought about how unjust this was.

Anand and Baloo were such good friends that they would accompany me every day while I walked from our village to school two kilometres away in Thana town. My elder brother Victor and even my younger brother Carlton, younger to me by two years, would march ahead and the slow and clumsy me would be left behind. Then Anand and Baloo, who used to be walking silently behind us, albeit keeping a discreet distance, would run and join me, saying, "Ay Samson, why becoming frightening, we iz there no."

They would fight between themselves to carry my school bag, paying no heed to my protests and grin happily as we took the long trek to school. On many occasions, they gave me a pleasant surprise by patting me on my back as I trudged out of the school compound after school was over.

I was scared of climbing trees in the village, while the other boys enjoyed the sport. Anand and Baloo were my coaches and guardian angels, who painstakingly taught me how to climb trees. Climbing to the top of the tall banyan tree in our village was a big conquest, which I achieved only because of Anand and Baloo.

"Be like monkey, Samson," they would say and then demonstrate how they used both their hands and feet like they were paws of a monkey to climb up – with your behind propped up and moving like a flexible tail.

I would climb the first bend of the banyan tree and sit there while Anand and Baloo scaled up till the top. They would slither down like snakes and lead me on to the next level. After nearly a month of patient coaxing and training, I was finally up there on the topmost branch to get a beautiful, panoramic view of my village. Anand, Baloo and I sat there for half an hour savouring the view.

The boys sitting below in the shade of the tree looked up, whistling and clapping. Victor and Carlton too joined in. Then Milton Aguiar said, "Pondya *utar, tu varun khali padhel.*" (Pondya come down, you'll fall down from up there.)

The boys laughed at Milton's wise crack. It hurt more because my two brothers didn't object to the dig, but laughed along.

We waited for five more minutes. Then Anand and Baloo led the way and supervised my descent. My heart was virtually in my mouth as I imagined that I would really fall like Milton had joked. But soon, I was safe down.

As soon as we reached the base of the tree, I saw Anand and Baloo rushing towards the boys. They hauled up Milton, holding him high in the air.

"Pondya *tujha baap,*" they yelled. "*Mang mafi* to ours friend Samson, *nahi tar tula amhi varun khali pheknar.*" (Your father is a *Pondya.* Say sorry to our friend Samson, or we'll throw you down from up.)

The boys looked on, enjoying Milton's plight. After a minute or so, Milton squealed, "Sorry, Samson." That was the first time that apart from Anand, Baloo and Dattya Dada, someone else had called me Samson.

Soon I became an expert tree climber. On the outer edge of the village was a cluster of tamarind trees. Anand, Baloo and I would climb any one of them and help ourselves to mouth-watering tamarind fruit. When we were bored of climbing trees after school, we would explore the town. We took along our *garandas* or wheels made of iron that we propelled with hooks at the end of long, slim metal rods. We were free and safe on the roads, as there were no killer buses or trucks on the town's roads, and cars were few.

In the good old days, my mother used a kerosene stove to cook. My grandmother, who lived in a neighbouring house, cooked on firewood and used clay pots. Grandma's food was very tasty – in fact, it was tastier than Mom's and she would always save a generous portion of her meal for me, because I was her favourite grandchild. We had no refrigerator. Water stored in earthen pots in those days tasted fresh like nectar. There was no television and we didn't even own a radio.

Those were the days when life was idyllic and simple.

The sailor boy

On Sunday, the 25th of November, 1945, a tall, strong, muscular, dark, twenty-five-year-old man wearing a red-flowered langoti – that covered his front, but only half his behind, leaving a generous portion of his firm buttocks visible – was standing in a queue at the public tap in Golvada with two buckets. His upper body was covered with a brand new, white, sleeveless vest, the muscles of his arms bulging.

There were other men in similar attire in the queue with the younger women dressed in long ankle length frocks. The older, married and more conservative women were wearing the traditional East Indian sari, of a purple-blue colour and a cotton blouse, with the sari's hind pleats tucked into the waist's centre.

The tall man Cipriano Pereira was not a regular at the public tap, but was giving relief to his mother Ophelia as it was his Sunday off day. So were the other men, chipping in for their mothers or wives.

As the queue inched forward, sixteen-year-old Mavis Moore made her first visit to the public tap, as the Anglo Indian family had shifted to Golvada recently from Byculla in Bombay. Mavis too was on relief duty for her mother.

As Mavis joined the queue, she made heads turn because she was quite a beauty with a perfectly shaped and well-proportioned oval face, light brown eyes, a flawless peach fair complexion, full rose petal lips, a well-endowed physique and an attractive smile that she mostly concealed with her arrogance.

Mavis had a regal aura about her, her impudent nose, somewhere between a pug and beak nose, pointing snootily up in the air. There were murmurs in the queue at the sighting of the new damsel in Golvada, daintily balancing in her hand a small bucket in comparison to the huge ones that the others carried.

"Sipee, see, see look behind," said Desmond, who was standing behind Cipriano in the queue.

No one in Golvada ever called Cipriano by his full name, as the villagers found it tough to pronounce. His parents chose this name when they baptised him as they wanted a high-sounding name for their second son, in comparison to their first boy who was simply called John. The East Indian Marathi speaking villagers, including his mother, called Cipriano 'Suplan', which seemed in no way connected to Cipriano.

When Cipriano looked behind at Mavis, he virtually jumped out of his langoti.

"Keep my place in the queue," he told Desmond, dumping his buckets on the ground, running to Mavis at the fag end of the long queue.

"I am Cipriano, and I'm pleased to meet you," he said, extending his hand.

"Huh," Mavis replied, sticking up her nose. But Cipriano wouldn't give up so easily.

"Madam, it is a tradition in our village to welcome new residents by allowing them to fill water first. You please take my place in the queue and I'll stand behind here," he said, grinning, a slight twist of mischief in his upper lip.

"Never. I don't take favours from naked men," Mavis said, turning her face away.

"This is our national costume, madam," Cipriano said.

"Now get lost and leave me alone," Mavis said, her face turning red with anger. Cipriano, considered a smart cookie with women, was silent. The grin on his face had vanished.

"The next time you come to talk to me, please wear your clothes," Mavis said icily. Cipriano gave up and quietly walked back to his place in the queue.

"Fail, fail, *porgi patli nahi, kai* Suplan?" (Fail, fail. Suplan, what the girl couldn't be wooed?), one man in the queue teased.

∨

The Moore family of six was having their Sunday high tea at 5.00 p.m. in the small living room of their two-room-kitchen row house when they heard a gentle knock on their door, freshly painted a lily white.

"I'll see who it is, daddy," Mavis volunteered.

She opened the door gingerly as the paint seemed still slightly wet. Standing at the door was an immaculately dressed man in a white naval uniform, complete with a white and blue cap and the emblem of the merchant ocean liner embedded on it. On the shoulders of the man's shirt were blue epaulets embroidered with a geometrical design in golden brown cloth and a button-like formation at the tip. The same type of golden buttons lined the front of the shirt. The sailor's clothes were either new or fresh out of the laundry. His stylish gleaming black shoes too seemed to have been just picked off the box.

He had a strong jaw line, firm lips that were neither full nor thin, sharp, penetrating jet-black eyes, eyebrows that were thick but not bushy, ears that were just the right size for a symmetrical, well-proportioned face that was shaped like a precious diamond. There was not an inch of fat on his face or body.

Mavis was known to be a tomboy who would whistle at the boys in the building where they lived earlier in Byculla. But if any boy took advantage of her openness and tried to hold her hand or make any sort of advances, she would box the boy straight on his jaw. The fact that she whistled at the boys, whom she found cute, didn't mean much, because she didn't find anyone of them man enough to match her spirit. But the sailor boy seemed like the dream man she had been looking for all these years.

She fell in love with him at first sight, without even knowing who he was. When she heard him speak she should have fallen out of love instantly too, but then her heart was doing too much of a pit-a-pat to change its mind.

"I have come fully dressed in my best clothes, ma'am, as ordered by you in the morning," he said. He wasn't grinning like in the morning, at the public tap. He looked very serious as he spoke, his voice well-modulated, his tone soft and polite, sounding like a perfect gentleman that any girl would like to bring home to show her mummy and daddy.

Mavis' father, Chris Moore rushed to the door, curious to know who the unannounced visitor was. Fifty per cent British, Chris was thirty-six years old, having married at an early age of eighteen years. Very fair, strikingly handsome, tall and well-built with grey-blue eyes and hair that was a shade short of blond, he seemed to tower over the sailor.

"Son, I believe in the Indian tradition of hospitality, so I welcome you to come and share some tea and goodies with us, though I must confess I'm a bit disappointed that you have come unannounced," Chris said, extending his hand.

When the sailor shook hands with Chris, he could feel the power in his handshake. This was the first time that Chris had found a person who could match his own crushing handshake.

"I'm sorry, Sir," the sailor said, eyeing the generous spread of a freshly baked cake with a rich dark brown crust, pancakes and frankfurters laid out on a table.

Chris nodded acceptance of the apology and led the sailor inside, with Mavis following behind, looking dumbstruck and smitten.

Chris' wife Candice, his elder daughter and eldest child Ivona, his son Jude, younger than Mavis by a few years and the youngest in the family, the six-year-old boy Paul, stood up to greet the sailor. Jude offered his seat to the sailor and rushed inside to get himself another chair.

Pleased with the welcome, the sailor introduced himself saying, "I'm Cipriano Pereira and I work for the Silver Line Shipping company as fourth engineer."

"Yes, now I remember you were the cause of a lot of mirth here after Mavis returned from filling water at the public tap," Chris said, laughing in a good-natured manner.

"Sir, if I had known that a beauty was visiting the public tap, I would have come dressed in uniform," Cipriano said, grinning, the slight twist of mischief in his upper lip, visible.

Mavis didn't notice it, because she was in a daze; but Ivona saw it and thought she should put the man in his place.

"So now you have come to show off your officer's uniform," she said, cheekily.

"No ma'am, your father too is a sailor I know; so my uniform is not to impress anyone here," he said.

"Then why are you wearing your uniform?" Ivona persisted, smiling her cute smile that brought forth both the dimples in her cheeks.

"Ma'am, none of my civilian day or evening clothes have been washed owing to shortage of water and this is the only decent pair of clothes I have," Cipriano said.

The Moore family burst into spontaneous laughter. Mavis didn't laugh, but smiled coyly.

When they had stopped laughing, Cipriano looked at Mavis, whose chin was buried deep in her neck, and said with a twinkle in his eye, "But it's good that I have come in naval uniform, because now my word may be taken as that of an officer and a gentleman."

"And may I know, son, what that word is?" Chris asked.

"Sir, you are a naval officer as well and you will agree that we don't like to beat about the bush," Cipriano said.

"Yes, except when we are talking to our wives," Chris said. That sparked another round of laughter from the Moore household. Mavis too joined in this time.

Cipriano didn't even wait for them to stop laughing, and went down on his knees before Mavis and said, "Mavis, I fell in love the first time I saw you this morning; so without much ado I ask you, will you marry me?"

"Yes, if daddy agrees," she replied, blushing.

This was the first time that the Moore family had seen the tomboy Mavis blush.

Chris laughed. It was a long, long laugh. After he had stopped laughing, he rose from his seat. Cipriano rose too. The two sailors hugged each other. Chris said, "I'm not saying yes, but I'm not saying no."

The youngest member of the Moore family had been laughing with the others, because the kid thought there must be something funny going on.

He said, cutely, "Sailor sir, when daddy says these words, he means yes, because he is always telling me, 'I'm not saying yes, but I'm not saying no', and allows me to do what I want."

Then the Moore family laughed again and welcomed Cipriano into the family, each hugging him one by one.

Why was I different?

This was the love story that my mother Mavis told us so many times over. But we never got bored of it, because she was a great story-teller. She was a great actor too. She would act out each person's part, imitating their voices and mannerism. And at the end of this true life story, a tear would trickle down her pretty brown eyes, splitting into tiny drops and flowing down her peachy right or left cheek, depending on which eye the tear came from.

And this was not the end of the narration, because the grand finale was always a tender love song in a dulcet voice. I hum and sing this song even today, because it was such a lovely, sad song. I didn't understand then why my mother ended the story with a sad song, when the love story between my Mama Mavis and Dad Cipriano was the stuff that romance novels are made of. But Mama would always say, "You'll understand the reason for the sad song when you grow up."

I am reproducing a part of the lyrics below:

A man came home late one night
And found the house without a light
He went upstairs to his daughter's room
And found her hanging from a beam

He took his knife and cut her down
And on her breast this note he found

My love was for a sailor boy
Who sailed across the big blue sea
I often wrote and thought of him
He never wrote or thought of me.

I was still a boy and wasn't really grown up, but yet I understood the significance of the song – that even if a happy story doesn't really have a sad ending, there's a lot of pain and sorrow in life. There are so many sad things that can't be explained. But as Father Francis advised us in Catechism class, we should accept everything as 'God's will'.

This advice I found difficult to accept, because I kept asking Jesus why he had made me so different. Why was I different from my father and mother? My father was such a brave, tough man.

I have seen him knock down three men singlehandedly, when they once tried to molest a girl in our village. On another occasion, my classmate Clarence's father was threatened with a knife when he asked his tenant to pay up rent arrears of six months. Clarence's father came crying to our house, complaining to my father. My mother tried to stop my dad from intervening, but he didn't listen to her and went rushing to the tenant's room.

The tenant emerged with bloodshot eyes. He was built like a bull. But my father who was slightly built in comparison to the bull wasn't afraid. The man flared his nostrils like a rabid dog, rushed inside and came out, wielding a big knife. Dad moved at the speed of lightning, and had to jump a few inches because the man was much taller than him, to give him a nice square punch. The hefty man dropped down like a sack of potatoes. Daddy jumped and stamped his knife-wielding hand. The man screamed in pain and released the knife. Daddy scooped up the knife, throwing it away.

Then he challenged the man to get up and fight him, shouting, "Get up, you *goonda*."

The hulk started weeping and begging for forgiveness, saying he would pay the rent by the same night. My father gave the man a hand. He got up and went inside his room, hands folded.

My mother continued to be a brave woman even after marriage. I still remember this incident that happened early morning on Sunday the 27th of September 1959, a day before my ninth birthday. I, the holy boy, used to faithfully accompany my mother for the first mass in Church at 5.30 a.m. Mama went for the first mass because that left her free for the rest of the day to do the household chores and cook the special Sunday fare.

As we were on our way to Church, a stocky man with a neck that might have been as thick as a man's thigh, came in our way and said in Hindi:

"Memsahib, mai is mohalla ka dada, Ismail hoon. Main bahut dino sey dekh raha hoon, ki aap savere savere, har Sunday kahi jaate hon, apna bacha key saath." (Memsahib, I'm Ismail, the dada of this area. I've been observing for a long time that you go somewhere every Sunday morning with your child.)

Then he grabbed my mother's hand and said in broken English, "Baby, you wanting my protection, no."

"No," my mother said and slapped him hard on the face. He left her hand and raised his hand to slap her back.

I had never seen a woman punch a man before, so I was stunned when I saw Mama punch him so hard on his nose that he was bleeding rivers of blood. He sat on the ground, holding his bleeding nose while my mother held my hand and coolly walked away.

I often used to ask God in the darkness of the night, kneeling before the altar in the living room, when everyone was asleep: "God, why have you made me so different – so clumsy, weak and such a coward – when my parents are so strong and brave. What is my fault, God?"

Winning strokes in one cricket match, thanks to my hero Dattya Dada, didn't seem good enough to obliterate the tag of 'Pondya' attached to my name. It was a crown of thorns that I was going to wear for many more years to come.

How I was christened Samson

Dattya continued as captain of Gold Winners Club because he maintained the record of winning almost every match. He retained me in the team and promoted me to ninth position in a year's time as my performance improved, though I never scored the winning strokes in any other match. My first match was my first, and was proving to be my last, glorious knock. Dattya didn't mind me not ascending the run charts, though he kept giving me refresher courses in batting.

He continued to shower his love on me, as did Anand and Baloo. The three brothers treated me like a king in Hill Mansion and offered me the only chair in their home to sit on.

Each time before I entered their home, I would take out my handkerchief and standing on tip toe, clean the board 'Hill Mansion' that I had painted so lovingly.

Dattya didn't ever force feed me a bajra roti again. But on occasions, he did surprise me with a tiny packet of chips that he had concealed in his ramshackle cupboard, specially for me. I would share the chips with the three of them. There were just a few for each of us. But it felt really good to be loved and wanted – and to be frequently called hero and Samson with such spontaneity.

Their love, indeed, made me reconcile to my suffering of being constantly teased with the disgraceful tag of a weakling or Pondya.

Their friendship was God's gift to me and it was the three brothers who gave me the strength to face my sufferings and I somehow knew that they would help me out of my misery.

Hill Mansion had become my haven. For me, it was a better place than even my home.

Their mother, Gangu bai was hardly at home as she spent most of her day cleaning homes or cooking for others. When not drinking off in some illicit liquor den a big chunk of the money that Gangu bai earned, Dattya's father Dondya lay sprawled in a corner of Hill Mansion, muttering something in his drunken stupor. I had never seen him sober and Dattya, Anand and Baloo would smile when I looked at him down on the floor and up at them questioningly. I didn't have the heart to ask my friends and hero why their father was a drunkard.

I had met their sister Shalu only a couple of times at Hill Mansion, as she too was out most of the day, slogging at people's homes, like her mother.

She was the fairest in the family, quite pretty in her own way, with a smiling face like her brothers, with large dark brown eyes, which were always adorned with kajal. On both the occasions at her home, she was wearing a gajra of mogra flowers in the bun of her hair.

Dattya had first introduced me to her in a mixture of Marathi and English, saying, "*Amcha hero mitra Robert Pereira, parantu amhi tyala* out of love calling for him Samson." (Our hero friend Robert Pereira, whom we call Samson lovingly.)

Shalu wasn't shy of me in the least as she was a good three years older. Extending her hand, she said, "I iz also going to calling for you brother hero Samson."

I was shy to shake hands with her. She snatched my hand and pressing it in hers, said, "Shake hands hero." Her hands were calloused and hard – much harder than mine – and her handshake firm like a man's, the result of scrubbing dishes, swabbing floors and washing the dirt off clothes by beating it with a *dopatna* (a flat wooden club).

They were a happy family and I never saw the brothers squabble. Dattya was always addressed as 'Dada' by Anand and Baloo and when he ruffled their hair lovingly and so frequently during my visits, it made my eyes moist.

Then Dada, who seemed to be observing my every emotion, would jump from the cow dung floor of Hill Mansion, where the three brothers were squatting and ruffle my hair and wipe my moist eyes.

"What happened Samson? Why iz you cry?" he would ask. "Samson always iz strong and not cry."

I was christened Samson by Dattya, when I was barely nine years old, after he had seen Cecil DeMille's epic film, *Samson and Delilah* in Prabhat Talkies that showed English movies in an early 9 a.m. slot on weekends.

Dattya being the eldest took on the responsibility of supplementing the family income by doing odd jobs since he was barely thirteen. As Dattya never had full-time work, he would use the free time he had to see movies, sometimes on his own, and at other times, escorting us. He didn't understand much of what was spoken in English movies, but they did help him in learning the language, in the same manner that we learned Hindi from Bollywood blockbusters.

On Fridays we competed with each other on seeing a new release of our favourite actors, the first day and the first show at noon, even sneaking out of school. But there was no way I could have seen *Samson and Delilah* with Dattya, because that would mean skipping school for the day. A noon show entailed slipping out at 11.30 a.m. and missing the two last periods, as our school ended at 1.00 p.m.

Interestingly, *Samson and Delilah* was a movie recommended to Dattya by my big brother Victor, because the captain often let his straight hair grow long like Samson. I don't know when Victor had seen the movie, because he never took me into confidence about his escapades.

But Victor did brag to Dattya that he had seen the movie the first day and first show at 9 a.m. for which he must have bunked school. He looked at me defiantly as he was recommending the movie to Dattya, while we were seated in the canopy of the banyan tree, sort of challenging me to complain to my parents.

I was wise enough even at that young age to not make that mistake, because Victor was as strong as a bull and his punches felt like hammers. I would know it best because I had seen him from early childhood knock down boys even older than him by the sheer power of his blows, whenever they tried to interfere with him.

His knock out blows sounded like 'daraam, daraam, daraam' and the opponent would be crying on the floor. So no one dared interfere with Victor. He was among the strongest boys in Golvada, but second only to Dattya, who was the toughest of all.

But my elder brother didn't really use his entire strength and power when he wanted to bully me, because he was a bit merciful in punches aimed at me.

He would even say, "You are my younger brother; go, go Pondya, I have forgiven you."

I can't figure out why he didn't call me 'Bhomya' like the others at home.

In my childish ramblings, I have diverted from the topic of how I got my pet name Samson, which Victor had wanted to gift away to Dattya.

As I was walking down home from school all alone, because Anand and Baloo had not paid me with their surprise visit at the school gate that day, I saw thirteen-year-old Dattya swinging from the aerial prop roots of the banyan tree, shouting, "Ay Samson *avaar yeh*." He was speaking the East Indian Marathi dialect and it simply meant, "Hey Samson, come here."

Dattya loved to be like Tarzan, swinging on the prop roots of the banyan tree. He had seen every *Tarzan* movie screened at Prabhat Talkies, including the very first *Tarzan of the Apes*.

I looked around to see if there was someone else he was calling, when Dattya took a mighty swing and jumped on the ground with a thud, shouting, "You Robert, you iz Samson, come here."

I ran as fast as my clumsy legs could carry me towards Dattya, who was panting with excitement.

"You iz my hero Samson," he shouted, ruffling my hair, driblets of his spit falling on my face as he seemed to have gone crazy with excitement.

"But, Victor said that you are like Samson; that's why he told you to see the movie," I said, confused.

"No, no, you iz the real Samson," he said, weeping as he held me tight in his embrace.

Samson wanted to be
Tarzan too

I should have been happy with the title Samson conferred on me by Dattya. But I was not satisfied with only one title and also wanted to be Tarzan, like my hero Dattya Dada.

However, I was not strong and brave enough to swing from the aerial prop roots of the banyan tree. Anand and Baloo were junior Tarzans in comparison to Dattya. So were my brother Victor and classmate Clarence and the other boys like Milton or Ashley.

For my hero, it seemed so simple to swing from the topmost aerial root of the banyan tree, holding on to the next one below and the subsequent ones, finally reaching down with the ease of a trapeze artiste in the Great Gemini Circus – an annual event that I always looked forward to. I had to forgo not one but two to three movies to go to the circus because the tickets cost thrice as much.

I felt guilty, going to the circus because I couldn't afford to treat Anand and Baloo to the show. I myself had to virtually scrounge and scrape to see it.

So I recall seeing the circus alone each year, though one year Dattya suggested that we go together because he had earned some money from a stint as a helper to a painting contractor. He also treated his younger brothers to perhaps their first ever visit to the circus.

The fun of watching the circus was multiplied because I had the best company I could have ever dreamt of. And in my joyous mood, I fell in love with so many of the young girl artistes that I lost count of them.

On our way home, I had told Dattya that he should try joining the circus, as that would make him a rich man. Dattya laughed and laughed, saying, "Samson, it iz not easy. Training iz starts from child."

"Dada, you are like Tarzan; so this would be like *bacha ka khel* (child's play)," I insisted.

"Samson, *tu maza barka bahu, phar bhola ahey, rey.*" (Samson, you my small brother, are very innocent.)

Then he ruffled my hair, which made me feel on top of the world. I often wished my mother and father would do what Dattya did. But then, at home there was so much of competition between us siblings, the three brothers especially. The two sisters were still too young to join the rat race. But Victor being the eldest always emerged as the winner. He was the first, and never the last.

When food was ready, my mother used to call us to the table in order of seniority, shouting, "Victor, Robert, Carlton, Debby, Sandra, come for food." Victor would shoot for the table like a bullet. Poor clumsy me would be the last to reach. But when Mama mixed up the order on rare occasions and took my name first, Victor would not move, insisting that the hierarchy be maintained, shouting, "Mummy, my name should always come first, because I am the eldest." Mama would comply, repeating our names in the correct order.

Oh God! In this childish enthusiasm to tell you so many things that were happening, I seemed to have forgotten the Tarzan story.

The circus with Dattya inspired me to try and become Tarzan. Samson was a title that had been conferred on me, like a nomination, but now I wanted to earn the title of Tarzan on my own. However, I thought that it was sensible and wise to begin practising at a safe place and height. And what safer place than the village cross, which though our meeting joint, was a holy place where no harm could come to me, I believed.

So the parallel iron bars, painted a shiny white, fixed over and around the village cross became my practice ground for turning into Tarzan. The bars on top were woven like a web at a height of around seven feet, just above the tip of the cross. The bars on top were placed at a distance of two feet. Bars were also placed from the top to the bottom, but only on the edges, leaving the four sides open.

This arrangement was ideal for me – to scramble across from one end of the cross to the other. The two-foot distance between each bar on top was easy enough to negotiate. And as I reached from one end to the other, I became like Tarzan, swinging to and fro, but at a safe height. After a month of practice, I became an expert at this cross bar game. From jerky jumps across, my movements became smooth and rhythmic. Now this had become my exclusive game, because none of the boys from Golvada considered it worth their while.

It was such an exhilarating experience. Not as good as Tarzan on the banyan tree, but good enough for me, given my physical limitations. I dreamt that one day I would reach the pinnacle of the banyan tree, once I got over the fear of swinging. While the other boys would boast about their exploits at school, I would keep myself busy with my exclusive sport. Sometimes, one of the boys would look towards me and say, "Stop it, you Pondya."

I would ignore their remark, but they would try to heap insult on injury, saying, "If you are man enough, go and swing on the banyan tree." And then they would laugh at me, all together. It hurt so much when they remarked so. But it hurt more, because Victor too would join in their laughter. Once I challenged all of them to compete with me and what I got in reply was a round of derisive laughter, peppered with the remark from Victor, "This is a Pondya special game."

"Ha ha ha ha ha ha…." The laughter that followed could have filled a page of this book.

But I was determined to continue my cross Tarzan act despite the ridicule, enjoying my sport. I had no cheer leaders, except for Anand and Baloo. And whenever Dattya came to the village cross, my swinging from one end to the other got a super boost, because he cheered me all the way. Then we would do the act together. It made me feel very proud of myself, because I was better than even Golvada's best Tarzan in the cross swinging game. Then the boys would keep their mouths shut like Egyptian mummies. It was my moment of triumph.

After two months of my Tarzan act at the cross, I had developed enough confidence to try my skills at the banyan tree. Swinging at the cross hadn't really been a challenge for a nearly 12-year-old. And I was still stuck with the 'Pondya' tag. I was determined to wipe out the tag forever by swinging like the others from the banyan tree, proving to be as good as Tarzan.

▼

Monday, the 30th of April, 1962 had been planned as the last day I would swing at the cross. The next day, on the 1st of May, Maharashtra Day, I would swing like Tarzan from the banyan tree. Unknown to any of the village boys, Dattya Dada backed by Anand and Baloo had already initiated me into the Tarzan act at a banyan tree in the woods behind Hill Mansion. I had been practising there secretly for the past two months. But I had also prepared a grand finale, my last show as cross Tarzan in the evening. So on the eve of Maharashtra Day, Anand, Baloo and I were the first to arrive at the cross.

Dattya said that he would keep out of this, but when we did the Tarzan show, he would be the lead Tarzan and I would closely follow him, like we had rehearsed in the woods. As he would swing from one aerial prop root and jump on to the next, I would hold the one that he had just left and swing. We had synchronised our moves to perfection and there was no room for error. I was going to erase the Pondya tag forever, for I had been trained to be like my hero. He would continue to be the champion Tarzan and I, the second best. The rest of the village boys, including my elder brother Victor would be behind us in the game.

Ha ha, I was going to have the last laugh.

So as planned, we waited for the crowd of boys to thicken at the cross. Then I announced, "Today is the last day that I am swinging on the cross. Tomorrow I'll swing at the banyan tree." My announcement was greeted by a huge round of laughter.

Then there was a chorus, "Pondya, Pondya, Pondya." Anand and Baloo shouted abuses. The boys threatened them. Anand and Baloo laughed at their threats. Anand said, sounding so cool but very menacing, "Come on, one by one, you boys."

"One fight from us and two down," Baloo yelled. I had rehearsed these lines with them, because we had anticipated that my announcement would be greeted with derision. None took up their challenge. It seemed they could only laugh, but couldn't fight. Then Anand and Baloo whistled loudly. That was the signal for me to start my last show as cross Tarzan. I swung from one cross bar to the other, in smooth rhythmic movements. After I reached the last bar, I was out in the open swinging to and fro with wild abandon. Then I turned my side and returned to where I had started and repeated the swing on the other side.

Each time I completed the last leg and swung, Anand and Baloo would cheer and clap wildly, whistling and shouting with joy, "Samson, Samson, Samson."

Now it was time for my tenth and last double round. The last swing was the most glorious one, which I thought even Tarzan would envy. I was swinging at great speed and I could feel the cool breeze brush my legs and caress my whole being, culminating at the tip of my hair. Sweat was pouring down my brow and my heart was beating like a volcano.

Then I saw stars…that you see when you fall flat on your back and your head hits the ground. Someone was standing astride of me. His face was a blur. I tried to move. But I couldn't. My legs and arms were seized with unbearable pain. "Mama!" I screamed.

Anand and Baloo were crying. I screamed as they gently made me sit up. Then, even in my dazed state, I could see his face clearly. Denzel Vaz was back from the Dongri Children's Remand Home. My elder brother Victor rushed towards him, fists clenched, yelling expletives. "I saw you unwinding my brother's hands from the cross' bars and flinging him down," shouted Victor. Oh! So that explained my fall.

I was expecting Victor to fell him down with his knockout punches, 'Daraam, daraam.' But Victor stepped back in fear, as Denzel whipped out a small knife and pointed it at Victor.

I heard the sound of two angry bulls, "Ahaooh, ahaooh."

Anand and Baloo charged at Denzel and butted him in the stomach. Denzel crashed to the floor with the impact of their assault. They then sat on top of him and banged his head on the ground. The fifteen-year-old juvenile delinquent who had been sent to the remand home following two cases of robbery and one charge of stabbing against him was screaming in pain and begging for mercy. Anand continued sitting on top of him, while Baloo jumped up and seized the knife that had fallen out of Denzil's hand with the impact of the attack. He flung the knife away. It rattled and hit the wall of the village well.

Victor filled in the place vacated by Baloo and hammered Denzel's face with his knockout blows. 'Daraam, daraam.' Each blow by Victor made Denzel scream. "*Maaf kara mala*," Denzel cried, begging to be forgiven. But my brother continued hammering him. Denzel was bleeding from the face. Anand and Victor relented and got up from his chest.

The muscular and stocky juvenile delinquent jumped up in the air and caught hold of Victor's neck, twisted it and dropped him to the floor by using his own leg like a crow bar, kicking hard on my brother's leg. He did the same to Anand, who was also on the floor in a split second. He was laughing at the fallen heroes. But his laughter was cut short by Baloo. It was incredible. Baloo had lifted Denzel by his feet and was holding him aloft over his head.

He spun Denzel around on his hand like he was spinning a top and flung him a few feet away. Baloo jumped on him the next instant and was squeezing his neck. Denzel was gasping for breath. Baloo let go of him and watched calmly with his hands on his hips as Denzel staggered up on his feet. Baloo turned Denzel around by his shoulders and kicked him hard on his butt.

"Goonda! Run run," Baloo ordered. Denzel followed the order.

The real Samson

🌿

The real Samson appeared from somewhere, hoisted me on his shoulders like he used to do when I was a two-year-old and began jogging with me. Despite the pain in my arms, perhaps because of injured or broken bones, I was enjoying the ride.

Anand and Baloo jogged alongside, huffing and puffing because they couldn't maintain the pace of the real Samson, who was almost thrice their age.

There were no motorcars on the road to slow down the jog, with me safely perched on top. Thana was an old quaint town of poor and middle class people who couldn't afford their own vehicles in those good old days.

As we reached Jambli Naka, Daddy took a left turn and a hundred metres down the road, ascended a flight of steep wooden stairs, without slowing down his speed. Anand and Baloo were close on his heels, panting.

As Daddy gently put me down on a narrow divan at the bonesetter's clinic, I saw a kind smile on his strong, dark and handsome face with a few drops of perspiration trickling down the sides of his temples. He was breathing fast but evenly, like he had just returned from an early morning brisk walk.

The small clinic had room for just a couple of chairs besides the divan. The bonesetter looked sombre as he began feeling my arms beginning from the shoulder downwards.

"Son, tell me where you feel pain the most," he said in a soft, singsong voice that reminded me of the nursery rhyme, *Humpty Dumpty*. "What happened, son?" he asked, gently.

I was in too much pain to narrate the Tarzan story. My Daddy didn't know anything about it. So Anand and Baloo who had been standing outside squeezed into the room with the intention of telling the bonesetter what had happened.

"*Tumhi kaun ahey*?" (Who are you?) asked the bonesetter. Anand and Baloo didn't know what to say.

So, I replied, amidst spasms of pain, "They are my best friends." I was dying to beat my chest with pride while I made this announcement. But I couldn't, because I could hardly lift my arms.

I could see the bonesetter raise a quizzical eyebrow. My Daddy sitting on the chair next to him smiled. It was kind of a proud happy smile, I thought. *Was Daddy proud of my best friends, Anand and Baloo?* I wondered to myself.

Was he proud that his son's best friends were dressed in dirty, frayed white shorts and tattered white shirts, wearing battered-looking plastic sandals that seemed to have been run over by a heavy truck?

Anand and Baloo, like two loving brothers, always wore identical clothes, which they never washed for several weeks for two reasons. First, they feared that the clothes would wear off. Second, there was not enough water to wash them.

The standing barb by parents to their kids in Golvada when they didn't change their clothes was, "What, you want to copy Anand and Baloo?"

But it was Anand and Baloo who were providing critical inputs to the bonesetter so that it would be easier to identify the trouble spots in my arms. Anand started the narration and Baloo would chip in whenever he thought his elder brother had missed out something.

When in a few minutes they had finished rattling the story of my fall, always referring to me as, '*Amcha sarvottam mitra Samson*' (our best friend Samson), the bonesetter seemed to know where to look for the injury.

"Relax Samson and look up," he said. I couldn't relax and stiffened my arms instead. "Nice name, Samson," he said. "Keep your hands loose and relax, Samson."

I thought Daddy would correct him and say that my real name was Robert. But I could hear him laugh softly and repeat after the doctor, "Relax, Samson."

That was the first time that my father had called me Samson.

"*Aay Samson, gabru nako, amhi ikde ahey na,*" Anand said. (Hey Samson, don't be scared, we are here, no.)

"Yes, yes, look at your best friends," the bonesetter said.

I looked at Anand and Baloo, smiling, love written in golden letters all over their faces; the white clothes that they insisted on wearing like a uniform, seeming to me like the rich flowing robes of King Solomon.

The bonesetter's touch was like magic. After a few pulls, tugs and twists, the pain seemed to have vanished. He had set my bones right. He applied a balm on my arms from the shoulder downwards, concentrating on the elbows.

"Nothing to worry, sir," he told my father. "He is lucky he hasn't broken any bones."

"Your fees, doctor?" my father asked.

"Five rupees," the sombre bonesetter said. Laughing for the first time in the evening, he added, "I am not a doctor, but a bonesetter."

He looked at me and said, "No more swinging like Tarzan, Samson, for at least two weeks to a month."

So there went my dream of becoming Tarzan. In fact, even a month after the fall I couldn't gather the courage to swing from the banyan tree or even from the cross.

Crowned Robin Hood!

Saturday, the 30th of June, 1962, was one of the most exciting days of my life. It was the day my elder brother Victor anointed me his partner in crime.

A couple of months after my fall from the cross, one afternoon I sat on a chair brooding in a corner of our living room in White House. That's when Victor came up to me and asked in a kind voice, "What are you thinking about, Robert?"

I was taken completely by surprise, because I couldn't remember the last time that Victor had called me by my real name. "You may never become as tough as me Robert, but I promise that I'll teach you how to be strong and smart like me," he said, a friendly grin pasted on his face.

I may have been really blind, for I seemed to have missed the hero at home. Here was my elder brother, with a healthy face that at fourteen years was already showing signs of shaping up into a handsome guy, extending me a helping hand.

"As your elder brother, I'll teach you all the tricks I know and make a he-man of you," he said, puffing up his chest that seemed to be growing broader each day.

My first reaction was to jump at his offer but then I recalled how barely a year ago, Victor had promised to teach me how to hang a picture but when I failed, he had put all the blame on me. I had hammered the nail into the wall with all my might, with Victor egging me on, "Come on Pondya, hit harder! I know you can do it; harder, harder."

I was up on a high stool, which Victor held tightly to ensure that I didn't fall. He had okayed the hanging, saying that the nail looked nice and firm in the wall. I had hung the picture frame, but the nail came down with its weight. And my father's prized picture frame was in splinters.

I had nearly fallen off the stool in shock and was sobbing in fear at the expected wrath of my father, though my mother left her mammoth cooking session in the kitchen and assured me, "I'll coax Daddy". As soon as Daddy entered White House later that evening, he looked up at the spot where he had instructed Victor to hang the picture frame. Instead of the picture was a deep hole in the wall.

"Victor, where is the picture?" he demanded.

Pointing out to me, Victor tattled, "Daddy, Robert pleaded that I teach him how to hang a picture frame on the wall."

I looked at my father. Tears were beginning to flood my eyes.

"I told him that the nail was not firmly in, but Robert was standing on the stool, and snatched the frame from my hand. Before I knew it, the thing had come crashing down," Victor said, putting all the blame on me.

I could barely see my father fiddling with his belt, because now I was sobbing in fear. My mother rushed to my rescue, but my father lifted me up under her very nose, flung me on the bed and trashed my behind with three strokes of the belt. That night as I lay brooding in bed, Daddy came up to me, slipped a tiny bar of Cadbury chocolate into my pyjama pocket, and said, "Sorry son, I lost my temper."

I tried to say something, but Daddy was out of the bedroom that I shared with Victor and Carlton, in barely a second. That's how my father was: quick in dispensing justice and punishment, quick in compensation, and quick in his entries and exits.

Then I heard a thud, as Victor had swung Tarzan-like from the third top bunk to the lowest one which I used to occupy.

"Come on Pondya, give me half the chocolate," he demanded in a whisper.

"But…but…" I was stammering.

"I have an equal share in the chocolate, because you have it because of me," he continued in a hushed tone.

"How?" I protested.

"You got that chocolate only because I allowed you to hang Daddy's picture frame," he argued. "Okay," I said meekly and took out the chocolate bar from my pocket.

Victor broke it into two unequal pieces, pocketed the bigger piece and swung back into the top bunk.

But when Victor offered to take me under his wings and make me a he-man, I decided to banish from my mind the picture frame fiasco and allow my elder brother to start training me.

The first lesson in becoming a he-man was to steal a papaya.

"You know Robert, I have stolen dozens of papayas from Aunty Patsy's tree," Victor said, puffing his chest up with pride. *Thou shalt not steal*, the eighth of God's Ten Commandments taught by Father Francis in Catechism class rang in my ears. I shut the commandment and listened attentively as Victor continued, "Robert, today you will steal a papaya and I promise you as an elder brother, you'll feel like a hero and he-man."

"Yes Victor, I am ready," I said weakly.

"Don't sound like a sissy; speak like a he-man," Victor said, holding me firmly by my shoulders. It was a real he-man's grip. I was proud of my strong elder brother.

"Victor I am going to steal a papaya and you'll be proud of me," I said, holding Victor's broad shoulders with all the strength I could gather.

He was gracious enough to say, "Nice firm grip, Robert."

I had never felt happier. Words of praise from Victor seemed like a blessing from God.

"You wait here. I'll be back soon," Victor said in a conspiratorial voice.

I waited in our bedroom. It was half past three in the afternoon and the whole house seemed asleep. Carlton was out on his long, lone-ranger walks that he took after lunch every day. Victor was back in a few minutes. He had a plastic plate full of red masala, mixed with vinegar and salt. My mouth watered as I took in the smell. He was concealing something behind his back. A wicked but friendly grin lit up his face. "Mummy is fast asleep, snoring and our two sisters are napping with her," Victor disclosed gleefully.

I nodded my head enthusiastically, as it meant that the coast was clear.

"We are partners in this crime, brother," he said, showing me the big kitchen knife that Mummy used for chopping meat.

I stepped back in fright. "What has this big knife got to do with stealing a papaya, Victor?" I asked.

"*Buddhu*, how do you expect to cut the papaya from the tree?" he asked, laughing, sounding like a real affectionate elder brother. Buddhu sounded so endearing in comparison to Pondya.

"Come on, let's go," he said, leading the way out of the bedroom. He was walking on tip-toe and I followed suit. Victor opened the front door and closed it behind us gently. We then climbed the stairs to the terrace at a quick pace. Victor skipped up. I was trailing behind. As soon as Victor reached the entrance to the terrace, he went down on his knees, laying down the plate on the terrace, carrying the knife with him. I was some steps behind, but kneeled down like him.

"We have to crawl towards our target, Robert," he said. "This way, nobody passing down the road will see us; you understand, no?"

The rough terrace surface was hurting my knees and elbows. But I didn't complain. Our crawling reminded me of the soldiers in the war movies that I had seen.

"Okay, action now," Victor ordered.

"Action?" I asked, confused.

"Put your head just high enough to see the papaya that I have chosen for operation today," Victor whispered. I peeped, raising myself a bit.

"Do you see a big, green papaya, right on top of the bunch?" Victor asked in a whisper.

"Yes, yes," I replied.

The papaya tree was in full bloom. Some papayas were a ripe yellow, while others were green. The top of the papaya tree overshot the parapet wall of our terrace by a few feet, making its fruit look a tempting prospect.

"Come on, go for it, partner," Victor commanded, as he handed over the big kitchen knife to me. "Do it fast; it's very easy," Victor said, continuing to lie flat on the terrace.

As I got down to the job, I realised it was indeed easy. The big green papaya was free of the tree in a minute.

"Have you cut the papaya?" Victor asked.

"Yes," I replied.

"Congratulations, partner in crime," Victor said, sitting up gleefully.

"Thank you," I said, sitting down, next to him, knife in hand.

He looked stunned and demanded, "Where is the papaya?"

Then the truth registered. I was supposed to have held the papaya, while slicing it. But in my fear and confusion, I had cut it and let it drop straight down into the neighbour's garden.

"Good, God," Victor said, under his breath, looking at me like I was a buffoon. I was expecting a smack across my face, for failing in my first crime with my elder brother.

"I can never become a he-man, Victor. I will always be a Pondya," I said, self-deprecatingly. I couldn't believe my ears when Victor said, "No, no Robert, this is your first time and you'll soon learn."

He ruffled my hair like my hero Dattya Dada did. A tear trickled down my cheek.

"You wait here, Robert. I'll get that papaya," Victor declared.

"No, no Victor; what if Aunty Patsy catches you?" I said, concerned.

"Robert, nobody can catch a he-man," he said. This time, Victor didn't crawl but twirled across on his legs and hands like they did in the circus. Before I could count ten, he was down the terrace stairs. And he was back at the entrance of the terrace in a few minutes, gleefully holding the big green papaya, rubbing the mud that was clinging to it with his shirt.

"Come here, like I did, twirling," he said. "A bit faster, Robert," he kept goading me.

When I reached the entrance of the terrace where my elder brother was seated, holding the papaya like a prized trophy, he shook hands with me firmly. "Congratulations, Robert," he said, thumping me on the back, like one does when you are back in the pavilion after scoring the winning run in a cricket match.

Victor sliced the papaya into neat symmetrical pieces. He made equal shares and we began eating. The papaya tasted really delicious, more so because it was stolen. When just a few pieces were left, Carlton appeared on the terrace, virtually out of nowhere. Generally, his entry was preceded by the whistle of some latest pop song. So when we saw his angular ten-year-old face emerge suddenly, busy as we were chomping, it seemed like an unwelcome intrusion. My musical brother was as sharp as a guitar string and immediately drew the conclusion, "Looks like you have robbed this from Aunty Patsy's tree."

"Yes, Robert was the braveheart who stole the papaya," Victor said, magnanimously.

"Don't tell me, Pondya robbed this?" Carlton asked, mockingly.

Victor was up in a split second, slapping Carlton smack across his face. I saw a red welt form across Carlton's right cheek almost instantly and his face contort into sobs.

"I am going to tell Mummy you are robbers," he said, wailing.

"Go, go complain, but never call my loving younger brother Pondya again," Victor said, grinding his teeth in anger.

Carlton looked more confused than scared, perhaps at Victor's sudden defence of me.

"What do I call him then?" he asked.

"Robin Hood, the great bandit," Victor said, thumping me on my back.

The golden gang

It was a proud moment. I was wearing the coveted badge of Golvada's daredevils – The Golden Gang. It was an instant reward for stealing a papaya: membership of the Golden Gang.

To tell you the truth, we never wore a membership badge as such. That would have been foolish and led to detection. It was a secret badge that we concealed within ourselves – in our proud chests.

Victor was the chief of The Golden Gang. His word was our command. Any order that he passed was considered sacrosanct.

The order of the evening was my induction into the gang. With my addition, the membership had swelled to ten. It was an elite group and the numbers were restricted. Victor was addressed as chief. The deputy chief was Clarence D'Silva, my classmate and stroke batsman.

That afternoon, after Carlton received the stunning slap, he was given the leftover papaya pieces by my generous elder brother. After Carlton went down the terrace whistling happily, Victor had said, "Robin Hood, there's a surprise waiting for you this evening."

Yay! Robin Hood was now my new recognised title and there was a surprise in store…a double trophy.

"This is top secret," Victor said, whispering into my ears.

"Yes, yes, of course," I said, my ears tingling with excitement.

"Around 5.00 p.m. today, I'll slip out of the house and you follow me quietly," Victor said, jumping up and running down the stairs.

I followed clumsily behind. In the stories that I read about Robin Hood, he was as fast as lightning, always escaping the long arm of the law. I was nowhere close to him. *But why should I doubt the honorific title bestowed on me by my elder brother*, I said to myself.

That evening, after the old clock on the wall of our living room chimed five times, Victor stepped out of White House. I followed as ordered. He slowed down his pace so that I could catch up with him.

Breathless, I reached the periphery of Mahakali Talao, where some boys, including Clarence had already assembled, sitting below a huge peepul tree.

Another surprise stared me in the face. He was a six foot tall Albino boy, with a big red freckled face, light grey eyes and golden blonde hair. He seemed like a giant. His muscles burst out of the white vest that he wore and his fair legs that peeped out of his skimpy shorts seemed as thick as the trunk of the peepul tree.

I had only seen glimpses of him, as he rarely came out of his home at the west end of the village, overlooking the Mahakali Talao.

The strong stench of animal droppings assailed my nostrils, as abutting the talao was a stable housing dozens of buffaloes owned by the Albino's family. Victor was quick to introduce the Albino to me, perhaps sensing the confusion on my face.

"Meet Casper, our one-man-army commander," Victor said.

"Casper, this is my younger brother Robert, but in The Golden Gang, he will be known as Robin Hood, the great bandit."

Casper laughed from his belly upwards. His whole body shook with laughter.

Then he didn't look tough and scary, as he seemed when he walked silently. He looked like a kind-hearted giant. He offered his hand. I took it reluctantly, afraid that he would crush my fragile fingers. But he held both my hands gently in his strong fleshy ones. They seemed like comfortable cushions.

Then Victor announced, "As Chief of The Golden Gang, I announce the induction into our gang of Robert Pereira, also known as Robin Hood, the great bandit."

Casper started clapping. It sounded like half a dozen people clapping. Victor, Clarence, Suresh, Neville, Quinton, Dunstan, Sebastian and Ashley, the other members of The Golden Gang, quickly joined in the applause. Following the announcement, there was a short swearing-in ceremony.

"Do as I do and say as I say," Victor said in a stern, official tone.

Then Victor raised both his hands towards the sky that was just beginning to get dark and commanded, "Lift your hands like I have done and repeat after me."

I raised my hands as ordered. "I, Robert Pereira, who will be known as Robin Hood the great bandit of The Golden Gang, hereby swear to discharge my duties to the best of my abilities and save me God if I fail," said Victor in a solemn voice. I took my vow in a loud booming voice, which was the strongest asset that I possessed.

"Now bow your head, join your hands and kneel before the Chief so that you can receive his blessings." It was The Golden Gang deputy chief Clarence who was now giving me instructions. I bowed and knelt down before Victor on the soft, soggy mud around Mahakali Talao. Victor laid his hands on my head and blessed me – not in the traditional paternal manner, but by making swords of both his hands and chopping at my head gently but firmly enough to register his authority over me.

He had already decided on my first activity as gang member, which would test my skills in deceit and crookedness, two most important qualifications to gain acceptance.

"I am not your elder brother in The Golden Gang, but your strict Chief and if you fail in the assignment that I have in mind for you, the penalty may be harsh, even expulsion," Victor said, his face as grim as the dark evening on the periphery of the Mahakali Talao.

The dirty dozen

The Golden Gang detectives had spotted their target of the day. The action plan was devised and was considered foolproof.

I was the executor of the plan. If I succeeded, my probationary period in the gang would end with immediate effect and I would be granted permanent membership. If I failed, I would be expelled immediately. The tolerance level for failure in The Golden Gang was zero.

"Action Robin Hood," the Chief shouted.

"Yes, Chief," I said.

I opened the door, closed it behind me and stepped out, standing in front of the house, nonchalantly, as instructed by the Chief and his deputy. I was wearing a white cap that cricketers don and a pair of spectacles with a plastic frame and numberless glasses that we had bought from a toy shop to disguise myself.

"Cake, biscuit, cake, biscuit," piped a sun-tanned stocky man, balancing on his head a big aluminium box that was as big as a trunk.

"*Cakewallah idhar ah jao*," I said, calling the man closer.

The vendor turned his head towards me with difficulty as the box of goodies was weighing him down. A smile lit up his weather-beaten face at the prospect of a customer.

He asked me for a helping hand. I held his trunk-box and assisted him in putting it down. I could see his dark face sparkle with joy and pride at the spread of his goodies, as he opened the big box.

"*Mummy kidar hai, beta?*" (Where is mummy, son?) he asked.

I hesitated for a moment, then recalled the coaching and said, "*Mummy andar hai, soh rahi hai; mere badey bhaiya andar hai.*" (Mummy is inside, sleeping; my elder brother is inside.)

Gang member Quinton, a hefty boy who had painted a grey-black moustache and dabbed his sideburns with white powder, languidly opened the door and handed me a huge straw basket. Without giving time for the vendor to take a second look, he shut the door quickly.

"*Bolo beta, kya kya chahiye?*" (Tell me son, what all do you want?) the cake man asked.

I ordered for everything that could fit in the basket, as instructed by the Chief and his deputy. The order included a plum cake, Mysore halwa, two packets of ginger biscuits, half a dozen patties, five *khajas* (a local delicacy coated with loads of melted sugar), six doughnuts and two big packets of wafers.

"*Kya ghar mein party hai?*" (Do you have a party at home?) the cake man asked, beaming with so much happiness that I could see the hair on his ears jump with joy.

"Haan, it's my birthday," I lied.

"*Ashirwad mera tum ko; hazaron saal jiyo, beta,*" (My blessings to you; live a thousand years, son), he said.

I felt a pang of guilt wrack me and felt like returning the entire basket of goodies. But the prospect of immediate expulsion from the gang made me banish the thought.

Instead, I asked, "*Kitna paisa dena hai aapko?*" (How much money do I owe you?)

He gently snatched the big basket from me, and sifted the goodies in them, jotting down each item in a mini notebook. When he added the total, he yelped with joy while stating the figure, "Seven rupees only."

I looked up at him, surprised that he had spoken in English. "I know little English, studying till eight class," he said.

I detected pride oozing out from every word that he spoke. In shame, I buried my chin in what I suppose was the cover of my thyroid gland.

He handed my basket back to me, and said softly, muttering to himself, "Seven rupees". That was big money those days.

"Wait, coming with money," I said in English.

"Thank you, thank you," he said, beaming.

I went inside and shut the door behind me. The Golden Gang Chief looked at me with pride on his face as he eyed the contents of the basket.

We quietly walked away from the rear of the house, silently latching the front door from inside. It was a disused house owned by Albino Casper's family. Located in the interior southern tip of Golvada village, the house was secluded, with no other homes in the vicinity.

Vendors didn't venture to that part of the village. But Dunstan, the lead detective of The Golden Gang had directed the cake man to the house, when he spotted him, saying, *"Last ghar walon ney aap ko bulaya hai."* (The people in the last house have called you.)

The cake man was a new vendor and didn't know that there was a trap being laid for him. Every new vendor had become the target of The Golden Gang, which used the subterfuge of the disused house for their heists.

It was afternoon and Golvada village was quiet. Through the narrow by-lanes of the village, we arrived at deputy chief Clarence's house verandah. It was a long eight by sixteen feet verandah, covered on three sides with wooden railings. Clarence's mother and sister were having their afternoon siesta, oblivious of the feast that we had stolen for ourselves.

The Chief, assisted by his deputy, made equal shares for each gang member.

Thumping his chest magnanimously, he said: "Everyone is equal when it comes to sharing our loot in The Golden Gang. I get nothing extra, though I am the brains behind the operations." We ate like gluttons and finished the stolen delicacies in minutes.

"I now confirm you as a permanent member of The Golden Gang," Victor said, looking at me benignly.

"Thank you, Chief," I said, bowing my head reverentially.

"You have really lived up to your title of Robin Hood, the great bandit," he added as a rider.

My first impulse was to puff my chest with pride. But my pride was dampened by the realisation that Robin Hood robbed the rich and fed the poor; but here was I who had stolen from a small vendor to feed the gluttony of The Golden Gang.

Samson was a crown that didn't fit my head, because I was not as strong as that legendary figure. My dream to swing from the banyan tree like the Lord of the Jungle Tarzan had been shattered by Denzel. And the decoration Robin Hood, the great bandit sounded so hollow, because I was just a cowardly thief.

The only name that fitted me to the tee was 'Pondya', I thought. I felt really sad. But The Golden Gang Chief lifted my spirit with good tidings, perhaps sensing the grief that was consuming his younger brother. "Robin Hood, considering your great achievement today, I grant you the privilege to nominate two members of your choice to our gang," he said.

I almost jumped with joy, as two names came to my mind in a flash. "I nominate Anand and Baloo," I said, reacting instantly.

"That's a superb choice, Robin Hood, considering the bravery that they showed in attacking that goon Denzel," the Chief said and gave his immediate approval.

"Thank you, Chief," I replied.

"Aye, Aye, Chief," the other gang members said. "We will then change our gang's name to The Dirty Dozen, which sounds more grown up and appropriate," the Chief ruled.

"Yes Chief," was the unanimous response.

Silencing Awaaz Radio

We ducked for cover as Aunty Lizzy Gomes, nicknamed Awaaz Radio of Golvada, accompanied by the cake man, tried to blow the whistle on us.

"*Badmashes* (crooks), loafers, robbers where are you hiding after looting this poor cake man?" We could hear her scream.

"Flat on your bellies and no sound whatsoever," whispered the Chief. We followed orders, breathing as little as possible.

"Come out and confess or I'll break all the bones in your bodies," she threatened.

Then we heard the sound of her tapping the road with her stick. You couldn't put anything beyond Aunt Lizzy. She was known to have eliminated stray dogs and even capricious cats with a single stroke of her stick that she carried with her, as she paraded the village like a beat constable. Aunty Lizzy had earned the title of Awaaz Radio for the distinction of possessing the loudest voice in the village. Awaaz Radio was the local loudspeaker service that villagers hired for festivals, christenings and marriages.

She would befriend all the vendors, promising them protection from so-called rowdy elements, preying on their fear, to extract freebies in the style of a corrupt cop. New vendors, especially, became her soft targets.

Aunty Lizzy, however, seemed to be oblivious of The Golden Gang's existence. She had so far failed to detect any of the gang's activities. This time, though, the threat of detection seemed real, as she had positioned herself close to the verandah, virtually baying for the blood of the robbers.

"*Kaisa tha woh badmash ladka?*" (How was he, that crook boy?) she asked.

"*Woh ladka, dhila sa, patla sa, topi aur chasma pahna tha; bilkul buddhu lag raha tha,*" (That boy was flaccid, thin, and wore a cap and spectacles; he looked like a fool.) the cake man said, giving the most unflattering description I had ever heard about me.

Despite their uncomfortable positions, I could see the gang members grinning. The Chief almost burst out laughing. But he controlled himself, for any sound would lead to Aunty Lizzy discovering us.

"*Arrey, sidha baat tum itna lamba chaudha kai ko bolta hai?*" (Hey, why are you giving such a long description of a simple thing?) Aunty Lizzy said. "*Woh Pondya tha kya?*" (Was he a Pondya?)

The cake man thought for a while and said, "*Hum Hindi may usko ponga kahete hain.*" (In Hindi, we call him sissy.)

"Ponga Pondya," Aunty Lizzy added for good measure.

Aunty Lizzy and the cake man burst out laughing.

I was gritting my teeth with rage. Indolent, sloppy and clumsy I may have been, but calling me sissy was like adding insult to injury. Now I was determined to avenge the insult to my manliness and silence Awaaz Radio, who didn't waste time in revealing her true colours.

She shame-facedly asked the just-looted cake man, "Show, what all you have in the box." The glee in her voice at the prospect of extracting her loot seemed to echo in the verandah, where we lay crouching.

Since they were within handshaking distance from us, we could hear the thud of the box as it hit the ground and the hinges creak as the trunk was opened.

"Wow, what lovely stuff you have!" Aunty Lizzy exclaimed.

"Pure *maal hai,* Madam," the cake man said with pride.

"Merooko aik plum cake aur char khaja dey do," (Give me a plum cake and four khajas) Aunty Lizzy said.

"*Ye lijiye* Madam," the cake man said, handing over the cake and *khaja.*

We could hear Aunty Lizzy's voice drift away, as she said, *"Paisa agley maine ka saat tarik ko milega."* (You'll get the money on the seventh of the coming month.)

Now with Aunty Lizzy out of earshot, we laughed softly, knowing well what this meant.

"Madam, *suniye…*" The cake man's words were left hanging in the air, as the beat constable had extracted her hafta and left.

❯

In the evening, I went to Hill Mansion and brought along Anand and Baloo, to be formally inducted into the gang to make it a complete Dirty Dozen.

At 4.00 p.m. the next day, I hovered around Aunty Lizzy's home, waiting for the show to begin. The rest of The Dirty Dozen, in groups of two to three, were waiting at vantage positions around Awaaz Radio's house.

Uncle Simon, Aunty Lizzy's husband, whose testicles were as big as footballs because of a strange hydrocele disorder that was incurable and declared too dangerous to treat, was seated on their row house's balcony. The bulge in his khaki cop-like shorts was clearly visible.

We had nicknamed him 'Ding Dong' because when he walked, he wobbled with the weight of the footballs that he carried.

Ding Dong was sipping piping hot tea and chomping at a khaja that his wife had extorted from the cake man the previous evening.

He heard wailing in the distance, but continued to eat and drink. Then the sound of weeping and the beating of chests in sorrow came closer and grew louder. Ding Dong almost jumped from his seat when he saw dozens of mourners advancing towards his house. The men wore black trousers and white shirts with black bands pinned in front. The women donned black dresses with black bands pinned in front as well.

Awaaz Radio rushed out of the kitchen, with some piping hot fried fritters to feed the ravenous appetite of her husband, grumbling to herself that it *looks like all the food goes into his big footballs.*

The wails of the mourners had attracted some sleepy looking housewives, children and old retired men from the thirty-odd homes in Golvada. They joined the crowd of mourners in a polite display of solidarity. The weeping and beating of chests by the mourners reached its crescendo when they were a few feet away from Awaaz Radio's home. With the addition of Golvada villagers to the outside mourners, the crowd had swelled to more than seventy people.

The Dirty Dozen now joined the mourners quite legitimately and formed part of the crowd. I pushed myself to the front, to have a ringside view of the entertainment.

Amidst the wailing mourners, I must have been the only one who burst out laughing when I saw the stunned expression on Aunty Lizzy's face. There was nothing left of the typical Awaaz Radio sound and fury in Aunty Lizzy.

She was silent as a stone when she heard the dirge. "Uncle Simon where have you left us and gone? Why have you departed without meeting us?"

Then the mourners suddenly turned silent, as Uncle Simon looked up nonchalantly from his plate of fritters.

"Uncle Simon, you are here, alive? But we received a message through your brother-in-law John, who had phoned the Sahar Church to say that you had died," blurted out one of the mourners.

Uncle Simon laughed with such mirth that his whole body swerved from side to side. The impact of his laughter on his footballs was so volcanic that it appeared that they would erupt out of his khaki shorts.

Standing in front, I now had a legitimate excuse to join in Ding Dong's laughter. Uncle Simon saw me laughing and summoned me to his side, saying, "My boy, come here and feel me to prove that I am alive."

"Come, come, touch your friend and tell these damn fools that your uncle is alive," Aunty Lizzy prodded me.

I hesitantly went up to Uncle Simon, touched him and announced, "Yes, yes, Uncle Simon is alive."

I now heard the eleven other members of The Dirty Dozen roar together with laughter and then clap loudly. The rest of the crowd joined in the laughter and applause. But Aunty Lizzy was not amused. She neither clapped, nor laughed. Instead, she announced, "I am going to kill that dirty bugger who is spreading very bad rumours about my loving husband's death."

"What are you saying, Lizzy? Your brother never phoned?" an old man asked.

"Yes, Gilbert. My brother John never phoned the church. He is in bed with high fever for so many days, and he can't even get up. How can he phone?"

A confused Gilbert elaborated how so many mourners had come: "No, no Lizzy. John phoned the Sahar Church to inform Simon's cousin Joseph, who went from house to house to inform all your relatives in Sahar village."

"Where is Joseph?" demanded Aunty Lizzy.

A timid looking, short, thin person wound his way through the crowd and said, "Yes Lizzy sister, Father Miranda came home and gave me the message and I went back with him to the church and requested him to phone other churches in Kalina, Vakola, Marol and Bandra to pass on the message to our relatives whose names I gave to the Father. I went around our Sahar village to give the death message."

"You are still saying, 'death message', you idiot," Aunty Lizzy said, flaring her nostrils angrily.

"But sister Lizzy, it's not my fault. You can ask Father Miranda, if you think I am telling lies," Joseph said, sounding hurt.

"Wait, I'm coming back," Aunty Lizzy said and went stomping inside.

She was back in a few minutes with her brother John, coughing noisily as he walked. He was holding Aunty Lizzy's shoulder for support. He looked gaunt with red eyes that were watering, a muffler wrapped around his head, though it was summer.

"What happened? Why are you all here?" asked Uncle John.

"Never mind, John. Come, I'll take you in and you rest," Aunty Lizzy said, rubbing his head affectionately.

She turned around and addressing me said, "You bring your Uncle Simon in and tell these people to go back home."

The crowd of mourners and the curious onlookers from my village began walking away, muttering among themselves.

Uncle Simon held my hand as he waddled into his home. I should have been ashamed of myself; the good, holy boy that I was, scoring the highest marks in religion, but my revenge agenda was still unfinished.

My act of helping Uncle Simon into the house gave me the chance to leave behind my signature in Aunty Lizzy's home. While I led Uncle Simon to a chair in the living room, I dug into my pocket, took out a sheet of paper and left it on the centre table.

The plan had been to surreptitiously fling this paper into their balcony. But now I got the chance to place it nicely on the centre table. When Aunty Lizzy came to the living room after guiding her brother back to bed, she saw the paper, picked it up and tried to read it.

Being semiliterate, she passed on the paper to Uncle Simon who looked confused as he read out, "Ponga Pondya Strikes. Silences Awaaz Radio Aunty Lizzy."

"What Ponga Pondya? The one who robbed the poor cake man?" Aunty Lizzy asked, looking stupefied.

I asked innocently, enjoying myself ever more, "Who is Ponga Pondya?"

"Not you, definitely not you," she said, aware as she was of my nickname Pondya. "You are Pondya, but a good boy," she said, certifying me innocent.

❤

You might have guessed who made that call about Uncle Simon's death to the Sahar Church. But for the record, I have to tell you, it was me, accompanied by the Chief and his deputy. We looked up the number of Sahar Church from the telephone directory that was in the phone booth of the Thana post office.

When we got the connection, the parish priest was called. I covered the mouthpiece with a handkerchief to make my voice sound grownup and conveyed the sad news, identifying myself as John D'Penha, brother-in-law of Simon Gomes.

"Father, please inform Joseph Gomes, Simon's first cousin," I said. I had met Joseph once when he came to visit Uncle Simon, and luckily remembered his name.

The sweet revenge against Awaaz Radio – for daring to cross the path of The Dirty Dozen and tagging the more insulting Ponga

Pondya to me – was my brainwave that every member of the gang had agreed was brilliant.

When I had announced my action plan for revenge against Aunty Lizzy, the Chief said, "You are a genius, Robin Hood, the great bandit. I think you should become our key planner and strategist, helping me with your most intelligent inputs." I had never received such lavish praise from my elder brother.

I was moving up notches in The Dirty Dozen gang, which was now my only hope to expel the humiliating Pondya tag attached to me.

On the evening after the successful silencing of Awaaz Radio, sitting around the peepul tree facing the Mahakali Talao, the Chief assessed our successful track record and declared, "Boys, The Dirty Dozen rocks."

Samson rises

The Chief decided to crown me joint deputy chief on par with Clarence in recognition of my checkmating our key adversary Aunty Lizzy.

We had planned a small celebration under the peepul tree in front of Mahakali Talao to mark my coronation. Except for Anand and Baloo, the rest of us pooled in altogether two rupees for the event.

In a run-up to the crowning, the Chief mandated that we should first test the soundness of my camouflage so that we could strike again if the opportunity arose to loot another new vendor. The test was that I should buy the delicacies for our celebration from the same cake man to see if he recognised me. There was the risk factor in that he might just recall the incident when he saw me, though I would now approach him without the makeup of white cap and spectacles.

But then as the Chief said, "A gang grows in proportion to the risks that it takes."

So, there I was at the cross in the centre of Golvada, waiting for the cake man to arrive on his rounds. My gang members, who had promised to come to my rescue if the cake man recognised me, were watching the drama from nearby, seated under the munificent shade of the ancient banyan tree.

The sun was still shining bright. I had to use both my hands to cover my forehead and shade my eyes from the glare of the sun. When I heard the cake man in the distance, more than a hundred metres away, calling customers with a staccato "cake, biscuit", I felt a gentle tremor in my chest – the kind that you experience when the teacher is about to announce results.

When he was close to the cross, I hailed him in my booming voice. He smiled the same smile that I had seen when I had looted him. It was so friendly and kind that I felt pangs of guilt cruising through my entire being.

"*Haath dijiye, beta,*" he said, pointing to the tip of his trunk of goodies, asking me to extend a hand to help him put it down.

"Tell me what you wanting?" he asked.

I pointed to a plum cake, a giant packet of wafers and two packets of cream cracker biscuits. He made a quick mental calculation and said, "One rupee and ninety paise."

I handed over the entire lot of coins totalling two rupees that I was carrying in my pocket. He counted the money and returned ten paise.

He packed the delicacies in a paper packet. As I held the packet, he grinned at the successful completion of the sale. I grinned back, satisfied that I had passed the test given by the Chief. He closed his trunk and indicated that I should help him place it back on the crown of his head. Then he suddenly changed his mind and opened his trunk again.

Wearing a conspiratorial smile on his face, he dipped his hand into his trunk and handed me two khajas.

"This special present for you," he said, in English that would have been perfect except for the missing verb and article.

I was reluctant to accept it. But he insisted, saying, "You nice boy."

I shoved the khajas in the paper packet and waited for him to indicate that I should help him lift the trunk. But he stood still, looking me straight in the eye.

God, he seems to have recognised me, I thought.

But his warm smile put my fears at rest. However, the next instant he delivered a bouncer that I desperately tried to avoid by virtually ducking my head.

"You nice and smart, good dress boy," he said.

I didn't doubt that I was smartly dressed, because I had been advised by the Chief to wear my Sunday mass clothes for the coronation ceremony. So, a boy with black, terry cotton short pants and a sky-blue terylene shirt, complemented by white sneakers that cricketers wear, would qualify as well-dressed.

"Come, you be my friend," he said, extending his hand that seemed calloused, because of the tough life he led.

I took his hand and shook it as firmly as I could.

Then he blurted out, "You helping me…this poor cake man in finding Ponga Pondya from your village who robbed me."

When I heard the phrase Ponga Pondya, I could almost feel a nerve in my forehead make a clicking sound. My first reaction was to return the khajas. But then I quickly regained my composure when I realised that the cake man had, in fact, absolved me of the charge of robbery and had indirectly obliterated the tag of Ponga Pondya, by asking my help in finding him. I was not a Ponga Pondya anymore! The thought made me so proud and happy.

And, it was now proved beyond doubt that as the to-be-crowned joint deputy chief of The Dirty Dozen gang, I had come out with flying colours in the camouflage test.

When I returned to the Gang, the Chief shouted, "Yay, yay, Robin Hood, aka Samson."

"Yay, yay, Robin Hood, aka Samson," the rest of the gang echoed.

Then the Chief put a red tilak on my forehead, declaring, "I appoint you joint deputy chief of The Dirty Dozen."

As we bit into the paid for feast and the complimentary khajas divided into twelve small bits, the Chief announced, "Robin Hood will be dropped from the new joint deputy's name and he shall be called just Samson."

I bowed my head in acknowledgment. And the Chief declared, "Samson has risen."

Samson falls

The five-kilometre trek from our village Golvada to Pokhran on the outskirts of Thana was so tough that it burst the bubble of my rise.

I was freed of the Ponga Pondya tag and officially declared Samson by The Dirty Dozen Chief. But the dropping of my nickname and the embellishment of a title didn't give me the stamina and speed to walk briskly across the winding, ascending dirt road to the hilly Pokhran area.

If I wasn't the gang's deputy chief and the star rogue, they would have left me behind or asked me to go home. But now I could see the Chief, the other deputy chief and the commander-in-chief Casper, deliberately slow their speed to keep pace with me.

And my best friends Anand and Baloo pretended that they too were exhausted and even walked a few paces behind me, just to make me feel nice. My special sports shoes that Mama had gifted to me on my birthday should have facilitated my walk and given me an advantage over the other gang members. Some of the ordinary members were even wearing rubber slippers, but they were quicker because they had greater power in their legs.

Good grooming can make even ordinary looking people appear like smart gentlemen, my English teacher used to tell me. But as I struggled towards Pokhran hills, the words of my PT teacher when I was around nine years came ringing back to me: "Robert, you wear the best PT shoes, but in any physical exercise, your performance is the worst in class."

I wanted to be strong, mean and dirty like the other boys. But who would give me the strength to be really powerful – to walk briskly, to trek, to run, like all the other boys of my age? With these questions weighing down heavily on me, we had reached the Pokhran hills area. But there was more climbing and walking to be done…along the water pipeline to reach the bunch of jamun trees, whose yummy dark blue fruit was the target of The Dirty Dozen. I had never seen such big succulent jamuns before, almost the size of my palm. We had a dozen plastic packets – one for each gang member – to fill with jamuns.

The Chief took the lead and scaled up a tall tree with the agility of a monkey to pluck the fruit. Others followed the Chief's example, but the fastest in the ascent were Anand and Baloo. I was a poor climber because of the lack of agility and power in my feet. So, the Chief instructed me and three other gang members to stay below and collect the jamuns that they plucked and threw to the ground.

Despite his bulk, Casper sprung up the tree like an orangutan. Considering that he had big hands, his haul and throw of jamuns was massive. In fifteen minutes flat, the dozen plastic bags were full with the jamuns. Each of the four collectors held three bags. We were waiting for the climbers to descend so that we could make our quiet getaway.

But we were startled by Casper who had slid from the top in such a mighty hurry that he snapped a couple of branches with the weight of his huge frame. As the Albino used to blink with his grey eyes, seeming that he was looking through you rather than looking at you, I often thought that he had poor vision. However, he proved me wrong, for he was the first to spot tribal men at some distance, rushing towards the cluster of jamun trees, dangerously waving their choppers and sickles.

"Run, run everybody, run! They are coming for us with dangerous weapons," Casper yelled, as he landed on the ground near us with a heavy thud.

The climbers were down in a few seconds, snatching their share of the loot from us collectors. The gang jumped across the pipeline towards the uneven ground, because running from the attackers, who were actually protectors of their produce, would be difficult on the narrow pipeline. I was virtually dragged over to the other side of the pipeline by Anand and Baloo when they realised that I had been left behind, while the others were already virtually running for their life.

Baloo took my packet of jamuns from me, probably sensing that it would then be easier for me to run. But my clumsy legs were not carrying me fast enough. I was the last among the escapees. The dark, langoti-clad bare-chested men with their weapons were closing in. The distance between them and me was barely a hundred feet.

Anand ran about fifteen feet backwards towards me, flinging away his packet of jamuns, so that he could use both his arms, and his legs, to speed his run. He lifted me like I was a child and placed me on his broad shoulders. Anand was a year-and-a-half older than me, but much taller, and, of course, stronger. I was thin and lightweight. Anand soon caught up with Baloo, who was waiting for us, ten feet away. He had soon sprinted away, with me rocking to and fro on his shoulders. The lead that he had lost, compared to the other gang members, was being narrowed down. But after running for a few hundred metres, Anand was exhausted.

He placed me on the shoulders of the stocky and strong Baloo, who was a few inches shorter than me. Baloo was faster on his feet than Anand, despite the burden of me on his shoulders. He even overtook Anand.

We could still hear the owners of the jamun trees screaming, "*Chor, chor, tyanna pakda!*" (Robbers, robbers, catch them!)

When Baloo too got tired, he gently put me down from his shoulders. Then each held one of my hands, and the three of us ran together. Their friendly, loving hands seemed to have given speed and power to my clumsy legs, for I was running fast, almost like a sprinter in a race. We soon caught up with the gang. I maintained the pace of my run, as my best friends Anand and Baloo continued to hold my hands till we reached the safety of Golvada village.

Samson dies, but
Robert learns to fly!

🌿

I had never seen my hero Dattya Dada look so worried. His eyes were red and there were small pouches below them. As I laboured up the steep hillock on which Hill Mansion had been built, I could see Dattya pacing up and down in front of his house.

I was responding to a summons from Dattya conveyed by Anand and Baloo, who were waiting outside St John The Evangelist School compound for me, the day after the Pokhran incident, looking very anxious.

"Dada wanting to see you, az we telling for him what iz happening in Pokhran," Anand had said, looking down guiltily.

So, without even changing my school uniform, I had sneaked out of home and rushed towards Hill Mansion, as fast as my clumsy legs could carry me.

As soon as Dattya spotted me, he came running towards me and hugged me. I could see his forehead crease with worry as he looked at me. Suddenly, my hero broke down and cried, sitting on the ground. My best friends Anand and Baloo came running out of Hill Mansion. The two brothers lifted their elder brother from the ground. I gently wiped his tears with my fingers. Then I lifted the long locks of hair on his forehead and swept them back.

Dattya loved to grow his hair long in keeping with the fashion of the times. But as youngsters in school, we were not allowed to keep long hair and Mummy made sure that I cut my hair on time. But I always asked the barber to keep the front hair longer so that I could apply Brylcreem gel to it and make it into a puff in the style of my favourite actor Dev Anand.

We shared the same favourite actor, but Dattya couldn't comb his hair like him, because his soft, straight hair fell over his forehead. So, he grew his hair like the Beatles, as did many boys in the '60s.

Dattya always carried a big comb in his pocket. He would keep combing his hair to ensure that his long hair didn't look untidy. But now as I looked at him, I realised that my hero had not even combed his hair.

He looked so sad and unkempt that I decided that I would do anything to make him happy.

But before I could speak, my hero Dattya said, "The *khota* (fake) Samson iz dead today."

"What Dada?" I asked, startled.

He grinned, showing his neem-brushed, pearly-white teeth, the long locks on his forehead jumping, as he shook his head vigorously, declaring, "And, now, I going to make the *khara moti* (real pearl) Robert very strong and very fast."

Under orders from my Dada Dattya, I quit The Dirty Dozen gang. So did my nominees Anand and Baloo. We didn't need to submit any formal notice for quitting; we just stopped going for the gang's meetings at Mahakali Talao.

The Chief took our quitting of the gang as a personal affront and decided that he must have the last word. So, though the gang had never done any paperwork in the past, Victor issued Anand, Baloo and me each a one-line letter that was addressed to us by name and said, "You have been expelled for life from The Dirty Dozen for your cowardice and failure to carry out the activities of the august group."

As far as I knew, August was a month in the year. So, I had to look up my pocket Oxford Dictionary for the meaning of august with the 'a' in lower case and was surprised to find that it meant 'majestic'.

One positive outcome of joining the gang was that the deputy chief Clarence, who was my classmate, now became my friend. He told me during the school recess that the Chief had decided to revert to the old name, The Golden Gang, because, to use Victor's words, "The Dirty Dozen name brought back dirty memories of the cowardice and failure of my Ponga Pondya brother and his friends Anand and Baloo, the sons of a servant."

My English teacher had told the class that your blood doesn't actually boil with anger and it is just a figure of speech used to express feelings when someone is very angry. But when I heard these words said by my elder brother, I became hot all over and the tips of my fingers, toes and head were burning. Perhaps this was caused by my blood really boiling.

As I recalled my brother's words while walking home alone after school, I made up my mind that he had become my enemy number one for life and that I would have my revenge.

I knew Father Francis would be very hurt – I had never seen that saintly priest ever angry – if I talked to him about enemies and revenge, especially against my brother. He would have gently asked me to go down on my knees and ask Jesus for forgiveness. Hence, I was not going to tell Father about my evil thoughts, but I sure would tell my Dada Dattya.

When I told Dattya what Victor had said and showed him the letters of our expulsion from The Dirty Dozen gang, explaining to him the meaning, he grinned and shrugged off everything.

"Maza rakta raga saha ukalatya ahe!" (My blood is boiling with anger!) I told Dattya. I had got the translation of the English expression from my Marathi teacher.

I thought my hero would be impressed with my spirited anger and knowledge of Marathi. But he wasn't taken in even a bit and instead said, gently, "Robert, you must forgive your elder brother."

I looked up disbelievingly. *How did Dada know about forgiveness taught in the Bible?* I wondered. Dattya said, "Sri Krishna bhagvan and Ganesha deva too telling we must forgive and loves."

Now I was really confused, because Father Francis kept saying in Catechism that Jesus Christ teaches us love and forgiveness.

And then Dada said, "Jesus too iz saying same to same things, no?"

"Yes, yes," I said, happy that my best friends and hero's Gods and my God were teaching the same love and forgiveness.

"I iz making you very strong and very fast, Robert," Dattya said.

I looked at him adoringly, wondering whether he had some magic potion.

"First, I teaching you how to walk fast," Dattya said, a serious look clouding his sun-tanned face.

I nodded my head, perhaps a bit weakly, for Dattya held my ears playfully for a while and then shook my head gently. His fingers were rough as he did hard labour at construction sites. Yet his touch was so gentle and seemed to carry with it some mysterious magic. But it was this mystery and magic that I found easy to feel and understand. Dattya's mysterious magic was nothing but unconditional love. There was nothing that he wanted from me in return.

What could a Ponga Pondya offer to a hero anyway? I asked myself, feeling really sad.

Dattya's next words aroused me out of my misery, as he said, "Robert after you iz learning how to walk fast, then you iz learning to run…and very *lavkar* (soon) you iz going to learning to flying, like a bird in the skies!"

And fly I did, as you will learn by the time you reach the end of my true story.

The true giver of Golvada

A man had been begging for many years in Golvada. Most of the villagers would chase him away, as he stood with his hands folded, pleading for money or food. A few would have pity on him and give him a coin or a stale loaf of bread. Then on Sunday morning, the 4th of November 1962, when the man stood begging outside the gate of our home, White House, he was surprised when he was invited inside by Daddy. My father was standing outside on the balcony, enjoying the cool late morning breeze. Victor, Carlton and I were standing beside him, giving him company.

That's when we heard his plaintive, high-pitched cry in Marathi, asking for food or money. Daddy shouted in Marathi, "Open the gate and come in." The beggar looked perplexed; I don't think he had ever been invited inside any resident's compound in Golvada. People would generally go out themselves and give him their doles.

Daddy beckoned him to come closer. He walked slowly and hesitantly towards where we were standing. Although he stood a few feet away, he smelled like a public dustbin.

He had dirty matted hair and a jet black shaggy beard. He was wearing what might have once been a blue night suit with white stripes. The night suit was now riddled with several holes and his brown canvas shoes may have traversed scores of kilometers, for there was hardly anything left of them – the soles were flapping on the ground as he walked and I could see his toes, with long dirty-looking nails, peeping out.

However, despite his unkempt, dirty look, he didn't look starved or weak. He seemed quite strong and I could see glimpses of his strong forearms and muscular biceps peeping out of his torn garment. He looked too strong for a beggar.

Daddy seemed to have read my mind, for I heard him asking him in Marathi, in a compassionate voice: "Why do you beg, when you look so strong and healthy and capable of working?"

"Will you give me a job, Saheb?" the beggar asked, smiling.

"Yes," Daddy replied.

My father drew out his wallet from his pocket and offered him forty rupees. The beggar grabbed the money and clutched it tightly in his right hand.

Victor, Carlton and I looked at each other, opening our mouths in surprise. Mummy too had joined us at the balcony by then, drawn out from the kitchen by the conversation between the beggar and Daddy. My two younger sisters, Debby and Sandra, were holding Mummy's hands, looking scared as the beggar was now grinning widely, showing his dirty yellow teeth. Mummy had arrived just in time to see Daddy give forty rupees to the beggar, a lot of money in those days.

My father asked me to go inside and get him a pen and a notebook. Daddy asked the beggar his name. We all looked on with great curiosity as Daddy tore a sheet from my notebook and wrote an introductory letter addressed to the security officer of his company, Nagar Dye Chemicals, requesting that the man be allowed entry into the factory. Daddy worked as chief engineer in the company. My father folded the letter and wrote on its blank face, the address of his factory in Kalyan.

"Get yourself new clothes and shoes, have a bath and come to my factory at 9.30 a.m. sharp tomorrow," my father said.

"Can you read the address?" Daddy asked him.

"Yes, I have studied till fifth class," the beggar said, smiling.

The beggar pocketed the money and the introductory letter and walked away, laughing.

It was 11 a.m., and with a few pegs inside him, Daddy was in a jolly and generous mood. My mother never interfered in my father's generosity binges, although this time she was really upset about Daddy splurging so much money on a beggar. But she kept her temper under control and even managed to laugh, as she asked, "You really believe he is going to come to your factory for work?"

"Yes, I am sure he will," he replied confidently. But Mummy didn't seem convinced at all. "You have children to feed and clothe, so don't waste your hard-earned money in these difficult times," she said and walked away in a huff.

❤

On Tuesday, the 25th of December, 1962, on Christmas day while we were busy celebrating, a clean-shaven, tall, dark man, dressed in black trousers and a white shirt, a red-flowered tie and gleaming black shoes, knocked on the door of our house. Daddy who was the quickest on his feet rushed to the door and opened it.

Standing outside was a tough-looking and somewhat handsome man. He was smiling like a newly-married groom. He had in his hands a box of sweets. Daddy invited him in and asked him to sit down. My father introduced the man to Mummy and us children. "This is my new assistant, Pandurang Shinde."

The man stood up, bowed his head, handed over the sweet box to Mummy, and left.

"I haven't seen this man before," Mummy said.

"You have seen him many times for the past few years," Daddy replied.

"No, I haven't or I maybe didn't recognise him," she replied.

"You would never recognise him," he said and kept quiet.

Then at lunch, when my father eyed the sumptuous feast on the table, I saw a tear trickle down his cheek. When Daddy had downed one too many, he could get very sentimental. I thought the tear was the effect of the booze on him. One tear was all that Daddy shed when he was drunk and emotional. Then he would say aloud, "Why am I crying? Forget it."

But now Daddy was shedding another tear, as he said, "I made a big mistake by not asking my assistant to stay for lunch."

"Yes, honey, you should have," Mummy said, seated next to him, stroking his head affectionately.

He looked up at her and shed another tear. "Would you have eaten with him?" he asked, wiping with the back of his hand the tear that was slowly trickling down his cheek.

"Why not?" Mummy asked. "Even if he is only your assistant, isn't he earning an honest living like you?"

"Yes, he is earning honestly, but he was once a beggar."

"What are you saying, honey?"

"Yes, Mooney, he is the same beggar whom I gave forty rupees to start a new life."

We all had lots of tears in our eyes, which fell over the rich Christmas food in our plates.

"I am proud of you, honey," Mummy said, sobbing.

"We are proud of you Daddy," we five children said, clapping and then wiping our tears of joy.

The youngest child, Christine, still a baby girl-in-arms, seemed to be gurgling with laughter in Mummy's lap.

'Mummy and Daddy
made you'

After tears of joy came tears of sorrow. The day after Christmas brought in bad news. Golvada lost Angel Papa, the village's mad man, who was the most loved person among children. But the most feared, and perhaps the worst hated, among devout Catholics.

Angel Papa was the richest man in our village. Or so we children thought, because he always had both his trouser pockets full of toffees. He roamed the village dressed in a full suit in every season, even summer. He might have had at least two dozen suits, for he wore two to three different suits every day. He was obsessed about cleanliness and bathed thrice daily. So, his face always looked smooth and shining. But his forehead had deep lines, like furrows in parched soil.

The toffees that he gave to any child he came across were not the cheap, local ones, but foreign-made sweets, ordered in kilos from a special confectionary shop in Bombay by his grumpy-looking wife. I had never ever seen Angel Papa's wife smiling. She had not much of a reason to smile, because the man whom she loved so dearly that she fondly called him 'Angel' had gone mad because of his generosity. However, she continued calling him 'Angel' even after he lost his mind. And he still called her 'Baby.'

She would dutifully come searching for him in the village, during lunch, tea and dinner hours, coaxing him affectionately, "Come Angel, let's go home and eat. I have made your favourite dish." Soon after he had his meal, he would leave home again, to stroll in the village's muddy lanes. Like his wife, Angel Papa too never smiled. But he laughed almost ceaselessly. It was a loud laugh of a mad man, without any reason or external stimulus.

Daddy was the only Golvada adult who spoke to him like he was a normal person. That was because being two decades older than Daddy, he had been his advisor when he was sane. In my father's youth, most of the villagers dropped out of school and rarely pursued further studies after they completed their matriculation. My father too would have been like them had it not been for Angel Papa, who inspired him to go in for an engineering degree and sponsored his education. Angel Papa was the first to become a graduate in Golvada and then a post-graduate in philosophy. My father was the first engineer in the village.

Angel Papa, a great philanthropist, shared his wealth not only with the poor but with the Church as well. Ironically, it was his generosity that got him into trouble with the Church authorities. Angel Papa had donated a five-acre plot of land to the Church authorities to build an orphanage. The authorities sold off the plot of land and used the money earned from it to renovate the Church.

Livid with this breach of faith, Angel Papa filed a case against the Church in the civil court and won it. The court ordered the Church to pay back Angel Papa the value of the plot. The local Church pleaded that they didn't have the funds to return the donation as it had all been used up. But Angel Papa was insistent that he get all his 'misused' money back. The archdiocese in Bombay stepped in to save the face of the local Church and compensated Angel Papa. But the archbishop sent a letter to the Vatican in Rome, recommending that he should be excommunicated for defying the authority of the Church.

Excommunication meant he would be declared persona non grata in the Church and no more considered a 'faithful' Catholic. He would not be allowed to enter any Catholic Church or practice his faith in a public Church or place of worship.

The fear of excommunication made Angel Papa very scared. He would kneel in front of his altar at home and pray to God for hours on end. He began visiting Hindu religious gurus to see if they could help him stave off the impending crisis, because the devout Catholics of Golvada and all the priests of the Thana Parish began shunning him.

Angel Papa met more than a dozen Hindu gurus and they all told him that he was being persecuted by the Church because they were jealous of his sainthood. They said that he was a reborn third century Saint Sebastian, who was believed to have saved Golvada from extinction by the plague in the year 1896, after the villagers had prayed to him. The real name of Angel Papa was coincidentally, Sebastian Pereira.

The gurus were not known to each other, making Angel Papa believe what they were saying as true. His belief was strengthened because he was tall, muscular and athletic like St Sebastian, who has a strong following among sportsmen and soldiers and is considered a 'patron saint of sports'. Now Angel Papa became obsessed with the idea of him being a reborn St Sebastian, who had been persecuted by the Roman Empire, tied to a tree and killed by a volley of arrows, thus becoming a martyr. Angel Papa got another grotto of the saint constructed in the compound of his bungalow.

The Thana parish authorities declared the construction illegal, because it was done by a Catholic on the verge of being excommunicated. The parish priest wrote a letter to the Bombay archbishop drawing his attention to the illegal religious activities of Sebastian Pereira. An angry Angel Papa stormed into the parish priest's office and asked, "Father Vincent Fernandez, how can you oppose me building the grotto of St Sebastian when I am the saint himself reborn?"

Father Vincent's ears had already been filled by Golvada's devout Catholics. Now the parish priest heard it from Angel Papa's own mouth. "So, Mr Sebastian Pereira, now I know it is true that you have been visiting Hindu gurus who believe in rebirth, when the Church doesn't," Father Vincent said, laying a snare for him.

"Yes, I have, Father Vincent," Angel Papa admitted.

"You have not only defied the Church's authority, but have also committed blasphemy by claiming that you are Saint Sebastian, and sacrilege by believing in heathen beliefs like rebirth," Father Vincent said. Angel Papa realised his blunder and that Father Vincent had him by the scruff of his neck.

Father Vincent telephoned the archbishop as soon as Angel Papa left. The archbishop made an international trunk call to the Vatican, which confirmed the excommunication. A few weeks later, a letter with the seal of the Papacy was delivered to Angel Papa ordering his excommunication from the Catholic Church for life. When Angel Papa read the letter, he went on a laughing binge that lasted for fifteen minutes. Angel Papa's five children rushed to their parents' bedroom to investigate the reason for their father's laughter. Suddenly, Angel Papa collapsed with the exertion of his unbridled laughter.

His eldest son Clive fetched the doctor, who gave him an injection to revive him. But he was put to sleep with a sedative, because when he awoke, he started laughing again. As soon as the effect of the sedative wore off, Angel Papa rose from the bed to laugh like before. The doctor shook his head in dismay, telling Angel Papa's wife 'Baby' Pereira, "I'm sorry Ma'am, I can't stop him from laughing; he seems to have gone mad. Mad people should not be kept at home, but in the mental hospital," the doctor said.

The next instant, the doctor found himself on the floor, as Mary had socked him straight on his jaw. "My Sebastian is an angel and now he is a saint," she declared. "He will never ever be sent to the mental hospital." The five children said in chorus, "Daddy is not mad; he is Saint Sebastian come again."

My father too believed that his mentor was sane. Daddy's reasoning was very simple. A mad person doesn't know reality and lives in his own insane world, my father argued.

He said that whenever he met Angel Papa, he would complain to him, "You know Sipee, after the Church has excommunicated me, I can't go to my daily mass, which had been a practice since my childhood." If he was really mad, he would have continued going to Church despite the ban imposed after his excommunication, my father argued.

As a child, I couldn't fully comprehend the complicated story of Papa's excommunication. But I was convinced that he was mad. Angel Papa would stop us as we passed him in the village, dig into his pockets and give each of us a bunch of toffees, after we wished him, 'good morning or good evening Angel Papa' depending on the time of the day.

After we happily accepted his toffees, Angel Papa would ask, "Boys, who made you?"

"God made me," we would all reply together. This is what we had learnt in Catechism class. Our parents too had told us this.

But Angel Papa would laugh loudly at our reply and say, "All lies you boys are saying, because the fathers in Church teach you all rubbish." As we looked at him, confused, he would wink at us and say, "Don't tell your parents I said this, but I must tell you this. God didn't make you; mummy and daddy made you one night."

When I had complained to my mummy about Angel Papa, she said, "Don't believe him; you know he is mad." My Catechism teacher Father Francis too said that God had created us and made us just like Him. So Angel Papa must be mad to say such crazy things, I reasoned.

When I used to throw this argument at Daddy to prove Angel Papa's madness, he would say, "Son, these are things that should not be discussed by young boys."

"Robert, you must love Angel Papa and be compassionate to him like a good Catholic," Mama would say.

"Yes son. I am doing well in life only because of Angel Papa; he is more than a father to me," Daddy would say, his eyes moist.

And when Angel Papa's eldest son Clive came running to our home to bring the sad news of the death, saying, "Daddy is no more; Saint Sebastian is dead again," my father broke down and wept like a child

❧

Angel Papa was not allowed to be buried in the cemetery of St John The Evangelist Church, because of his excommunication. Despite being offered four times the usual money, the hearse service was unwilling to bear Angel Papa's coffin, fearing that other Catholics would boycott them if they learnt that the vehicle was used to carry a 'sinner'. Even coffin makers refused to make a coffin for him. Daddy got wood from a local dealer and got a coffin made with the help of a local carpenter. Luckily, a burial ground had been identified for him in an old, abandoned cemetery, five kilometers away on the outskirts of Thana town.

Apart from Angel Papa's family, the only other mourners were me and my Daddy. My father asked the carpenter to join the funeral because we seemed to be short of people to bear the coffin. My contribution in terms of the distance that I carried the coffin was not as much as Daddy, but it was not so bad either, because my training under Dattya – to become strong and fast – had commenced more than a month ago. But more than my part in bearing the coffin was my role as a de facto priest in laying to rest Angel Papa.

As the coffin was lowered into the grave and we began filling the pit with mud, Daddy came up to me and said, "Robert, you act as the priest and say the usual words."

"Dust thou art and to dust thou shall return," I said. "God bless you in Christ, Sebastian Pereira. By the Mercy of God, may your soul rest in peace."

That night after the funeral, I saw Angel Papa kneeling on a red carpet in front the village cross. Angel Papa was not kneeling on the stones that he used to every midnight after the villagers had gone to sleep, shouting the Lord's Prayer like a mad man. Now he was praying in a soft, calm voice, smiling beautifully, instead of laughing hysterically.

And I now believed Daddy. Angel Papa was not mad. He was really a saint, even if he was not St Sebastian reborn.

The 'Saint' had blessed me
with a miracle

When I got out of the lowest bunk that morning, I felt a spring in my step. Was I imagining or was it real?

Victor had jumped from the top bunk and was making a dash for the loo that was in the backyard. As the eldest, he considered it his privilege to use the bathroom first among the children. But I strode past him, with long sprightly steps, opened the toilet door and bolted it securely from inside.

"What? How dare you go in before the eldest son?" he yelled from outside.

I didn't answer him.

"Small or big job?" he asked.

"Big," I said.

"What, you said big?" he asked, sounding like I had committed some major offence.

After a minute, he began banging hard at the door, shouting, "Hurry, you Ponga Pondya."

He kept hammering at the door, attracting Mummy's attention. She rushed from the kitchen to investigate the commotion.

I smiled inside, as I heard her scolding Victor, "Behave yourself."

"Mummy, he is misbehaving by going inside before me, the eldest son, when it is my right to be first," Victor said.

"Who gave you that right, Victor?" Mummy asked. She was beginning to sound angry, for I could hear her raise her voice.

"Daddy always says that I am the first, the eldest and so the best," Victor said. I was tempted to laugh the way Angel Papa used to. But I didn't have to, for Mummy laughed for me. Oh! When Mummy laughed, it was such a delight to hear. It was laughter full of fun and cheer…not loud and boisterous, just good-natured. Victor obviously didn't like Mummy's laughter, for he said, "Mummy, am I not the eldest with the right…."

Mummy cut him short and I heard her say, "Your father has spoiled you, Victor."

"You are taking his side, though he has taken my turn," Victor said.

I was expecting a bashing from Victor when I emerged from the loo. Mummy had gone back to her cooking in the kitchen and I suspected my elder brother lay in wait for me. As I stepped out, Victor charged at me as expected. But I dodged him and scooted away. I stood safely near my mother in the kitchen, preparing the morning breakfast. I looked at Victor from the corner of my eye and could see him gritting his teeth. I was hoping that he would soon be summoned by nature; and sure enough, he soon rushed to the loo.

It was an unusual school day, for rightfully it was our Christmas vacation. But we had a new school principal, Father Alex Pimenta, who was believed to be eccentric and kept the 27th of December a working day – Thanksgiving Day, in fact – after which our two-week Christmas holidays would resume.

As I got busy putting my school bag together, I heard the sound of quick footsteps approaching our bedroom, even as Carlton who was always the last to wake up, but the quickest to get ready, jumped down from the second bunk where he used to sleep.

I put my bag aside and stood in a state of high alert. There he was – Victor with his fists menacingly aimed at my back. I ducked, went under him and ran out of the room. He was close on my heels, but he couldn't get me.

Round and round I ran in the garden. All attempts by Victor to get hold of me failed. He was panting and I could see spit dribbling down his mouth. He looked at me like I was a ghost. That was perhaps because he couldn't believe what was happening. I was running faster than him.

He gave up the chase and went inside the house to bathe and get ready for school. And the bath that he had was 'double royal', which I knew was deliberate. It was now Mummy's turn to bang on the bathroom door, asking him to hurry up. After what seemed an eternity, Victor emerged, wrapped in one of the best towels we had at home – another perk of being the eldest – a wicked grin on his face.

By the time I got ready, I realised I was running late for school. Victor and the speed-dresser Carlton were already on the road. But as I glided on the road to school, I felt strange, as if this was not me doing the walking. I reached school a minute before the assembly bell rang. And I ran to the first row to sing the school hymn with a dozen other boys chosen for that 'special thanksgiving day'.

However, in class, I could hardly concentrate on my studies, lost as I was in thought that something strange but superb had happened to me overnight.

There was no Catechism class that day. But as soon as the bell rang to signal the end of school, I grabbed my bag and rushed to Father Francis' room, in the priests' living quarters, which was in an annexe of the Church. Father Francis gave me his sweet saintly smile when he saw me. But I didn't want to waste time and decided to come clean immediately. I knelt before him and began my Confession saying, "Father, I have sinned."

"Saturday is allotted for Confession, son, and that too in the Church premises, in the anonymity of the confessional," Father Francis said, lifting me from the floor.

I was hoping that Father Francis would break tradition and let me make an open confession to him. But he was a stickler for rules and would hear none of my plea, "Father it's very urgent, please, please."

"We can talk, son, and discuss man-to-man so that you can unburden yourself. Then you can make a formal confession on Saturday, which is just two days away," Father Francis said, placating me.

I got up from the ground and sat on a hard wooden chair without cushions, opposite him, while he reclined on the single sofa piece. Priests who had taken the vows of poverty, celibacy and chastity didn't have the luxury of ornate three piece sofa sets.

My words came out like a gushing spring as I said, "Father, I played the role of a priest and in the name of Christ blessed Sebastian Pereira, who was buried in an old abandoned cemetery, praying that with the mercy of God, his soul rests in peace." I then closed my eyes, because I didn't have the courage to face Father Francis.

I felt a gentle hand on my lap. The hand then touched the crown of my head. My heart soared with indescribable joy that I had never experienced before. The crown of my head was tingling with a strange sensation that seemed to lift it from its centre in my skull. For several moments, I felt like I was not sitting on the hard chair, but floating in the room. "Bless you, my son," Father Francis whispered.

When after some moments the feeling of bliss had ended and I opened my eyes, I realised that Father Francis had been kneeling before me, showering me with his blessings.

I held his hand and he rose from the ground, returning to the sofa, his eyes gleaming, his lips smiling interminably. I thought Father Francis would be mad at me for not only attending the funeral of a person excommunicated by the Church, but also having the audacity to bless him like I was a priest.

Then I nearly jumped out of my chair when I heard Father Francis say, "Son, you did all this in innocence and good faith, but I am guilty of blasphemy and treason as a minister of Christ, because I did everything in full knowledge and consciousness."

"What did you do, Father?" I asked, shocked at the grave charges that he was levelling upon himself.

"After he was excommunicated, I used to visit Mr Sebastian Pereira, on the quiet twice a week, hear his confession and give him Holy Communion, though he had been lawfully thrown out of the Church." Father Francis was laughing aloud. His laughter reminded me of the way Angel Papa laughed. The laughter we all thought was of a mad man…when it was really that of a misunderstood saint.

"And I blessed and consecrated to God the St Sebastian grotto that he had built, because I believed that he was right and the Church was wrong," he said, laughing the same laugh. I was really confused; perhaps because this was too much for a twelve-year-old to understand.

"You don't have to make a Confession about what you did for Sebastian," he said.

"Really Father?" I asked, sounding relieved.

"When you sailed into my room, all the clumsiness of your movements seeming to vanish, I knew that it was a miracle that only a saint could have performed," Father Francis said.

"Saint Sebastian Pereira has performed his first miracle and you are the lucky beneficiary," he added with his saintly smile.

My hero punctures
the miracle balloon

After the ruckus that my beating Victor to the loo had created in the morning, Mummy was careful to call out our names in the correct order of seniority for lunch. It required great restraint on my part not to cross Victor. I could have done it easily with my new-found swiftness.

Soon after lunch, without even changing my school uniform, I made a dash for Hill Mansion. I had never imagined that the ascent to the hillock leading to the home of the people whom I loved so much would be so easy. It seemed that I was not even running, but flying in an aircraft.

Whoosh!

I dashed straight into their hut, without even bothering to check if Dattya, Anand and Baloo were at home.

I nearly stamped on their dad sleeping right in the centre; it seemed he had passed out from over-consumption of booze and was unable to move himself to his favourite corner where he usually slept. The three brothers jumped up from the floor in surprise when they saw me descend.

"*Chamatkar!* It's a miracle!" I yelled, looking at their dad, hoping that I wouldn't wake him up with my shouting. Their father continued to sleep peacefully, though sweat trickled down his face and bare chest, like a light drizzle in the monsoon.

Anand, Baloo and Dattya rushed towards me, asking together, "What chamatkar?"

I was a bit disappointed that they hadn't made out the miracle from the manner in which I shot into their home. But that didn't stop me from babbling, "I can run, I can run."

And I ran out of their hut to show what I meant.

I hopped down from the rear of Hill Mansion towards the woods below. The three brothers were close on my heels and had soon caught up with me. As I quickened my pace to full throttle, the trio whizzed past me. No matter how much punch I put into my legs, there was not even the slightest chance of me catching up with them.

When we had gone deep into the woods and the trees seemed taller and the chirping of birds sounded clearer, the three brothers halted and waited for me to catch up. Led by Dattya, the three took turns in hugging me and then lifting me and placing me on their shoulders, to celebrate my path-breaking run in the woods. But despite the celebration, I felt a strange sadness engulf me. I had been happy cavorting into Hill Mansion and out of it into the woods, but I was sad that the three brothers still ran much faster, despite the miracle bestowed on me by Angel Papa.

Was the saint's miracle not good enough to make me the fastest? I asked myself, brooding.

Those who love you can read you like an open book and my best friends seemed to have seen the sadness creep into me. Dattya Dada too had sensed the disappointment in me.

And I felt sadder when I realised that the ones who loved me were the trigger for the sadness, after my bout of joy.

"Chamatkar! You iz running soh fast," Baloo said.

"*Kara* (real) chamatkar," echoed Anand.

My handsome hero looked the kindest and the most loving to me somehow, may be because I virtually adored him. When he came up to me, smiling, I felt like the sadness that was bottled up inside me was uncorking itself and disappearing into the refreshing air of the woods.

When Dattya ruffled my hair and pulled my cheeks playfully like an elder brother would do, which Victor never ever did, I felt that I was ready to run again in the woods…and it wouldn't really matter that the three brothers would still be faster – because no miracle is better than love, nah.

Dattya also explained to me that love is indeed the best miracle. *"Maaza dhakta bhau, prem sarvottam chamatkar ahey."*

"Yes, yes, Dada," I agreed readily.

"Tumcha davnachya karan, tumcha svatacha naveen atmavishwas ani svata sathi prem ahey," (The reason for your running is your own new self-esteem and love for yourself) he said, smiling.

I told him that I was running so well because Saint Angel Papa had blessed me with a miracle and that Father Francis too had agreed to this.

"No, no! You must not believes in chamatkar, but hard work, which iz making you strong," he said emphatically. "And now you seeing, how hard work is making the *kara chamatkar*," he added.

The three brothers were now crying.

Those were tears of joy…more blessed than any miracle.

A miracle begins to
take shape

※

"One, two, three, four, five, six…" Dattya counted. But he had to stop his count, for after doing six pushups, I fell flat on my face, which got covered with mud.

Anand and Baloo rushed to pick me up, but Dattya Dada shouted, "Wait! He iz no baby and he iz only getting up."

The brothers ignored Dattya's order and kneeling down near me, each offered me a hand so that I could rise from the ground.

My hero rushed towards his brothers, hauled them both up from their kneeling position and sent them twirling away from me. They tried to balance themselves, but couldn't, and fell on their sides like spinning tops that had lost their momentum.

Seeing that my best friends had fallen for my sake, I jumped from the ground and stood in front of Dada in a confrontationist posture, my hands on my hips.

My hero looked amused, smiled and said, "Very good. I know you iz angry and I liking this."

This was the first time I was angry with my hero. It was also my first experience of his being rough and rude with his brothers and me. Then I was taken completely by surprise when Dada pushed me around, challenging me to fight him.

"Come, Mr Chamatkar! Come fighting with me," he said, flexing his muscles.

The biceps of my construction worker Dada were bulging. As he clenched his fists, they seemed like heads of hammers and his forearms looked like the barks of trees.

There was no way that I could fight him with my spindly arms.

Anand and Baloo, who had recovered from the tailspin that Dada had sent them into, rushed to my side. They were flaring their nostrils like wild horses, jumping about, their fists pointed towards Dada.

"Come Dada, fight with uz, three brothers," Anand challenged my hero.

He accepted the challenge and before I could even count one, he had held Anand by his neck and tossed him down to the ground. Baloo jumped on to Dada's back and tugged at his long hair, throwing my hero off balance. As they tumbled down together on the soggy ground in the woods, Dattya had rolled over and was on top of Baloo, pinning him down.

Anand jumped to the ground and tried to pull Dada away from Baloo. But Dattya was holding Baloo too firmly to be torn away. Then Anand started hammering Dattya's back. Dada seemed unaffected. As Anand continued his attack, Dattya giggled, saying, *"Chaan maalish, mala deto tu dhakta bhau,"* ruling out the blows as massage. But Baloo wasn't amused as he was being virtually smothered by Dattya's weight.

"Robert, you also hit the Dada, and save for me," I could hear him squeak.

Me…me? How can I strike my Dada, I said to myself. But as the pitch of Baloo's screams rose and he began pleading, "Pleeze, pleeze," I could control myself no longer. I joined Anand in hammering Dada's back. The joint onslaught made him utter, *"Aai ga!"* (Oh mummy!) He let go of the grip on Baloo and stood up, holding his hands up, saying, "I iz losing fight with three young goondas."

He shook my hand, saying, "Your hands iz soon becoming strong like iron."

Then he shook hands with Anand and Baloo too and said, *"Abhinandan, tumhi teen fight jinkle,"* congratulating us for our victory over him.

"Thank you," we said together.

Then Dada sprung a surprise at me, announcing. "Now, Robert iz doing six pushups again and not falling on the mud."

"Yez, Yez," Anand and Baloo gave their approval.

And I did it…six pushups, without falling; lifting myself neatly off the ground as I finished. We repeated the pushups and the wrestling match between us 'brothers' the next day. Then it became a daily routine.

When I used to return home, I had a tough time explaining to Mummy why my clothes were soiled and soaked in mud. So, I would sneak into the house and quickly change my clothes, dumping the soiled ones in the basket assigned for dirty clothes.

I enjoyed doing the pushups, rolling on the mud, the friendly wrestling matches and joining in boxing Dada's back till he gave up his hold on the person whom he had held captive in his strong grip. But he still treated me with kid's gloves and never granted me the honour of wrestling with him like he did with Anand and Baloo.

I was praying for that miracle to happen soon. The day Dada would consider me fit enough to wrestle with him was the miracle that I yearned for. But the prospect seemed distant. However, two months after my first 'confrontation' with my hero, I seemed closer to my dream miracle.

When the brothers sat on the mud in the backyard of Hill Mansion, passing each other bajra rotis, onions and chillies, I grabbed one roti, and an onion and wolfed it up. Then I grabbed a second roti and added a chilli for taste to the onion.

Now I felt strong and halfway through the qualification for a wrestling match with Dada.

The miracle was beginning to take shape.

The tough miracle crust

※

"No," yelled Dattya. "No, you iz not going home till you iz finizing seven pushups."

It was a shame – a real shame that I had been stuck on six pushups for the last two months.

When I stopped after I had reached six and just couldn't do more, he continued standing on the soft mud in the woods behind Hill Mansion and counted till ten, perhaps in the hope that I should have at least reached that figure by then.

Anand and Baloo who had been doing their pushups a little distance from me, stopped after doing their over dozen pushups, and rushed towards me. Dada smiled, shook his head and sat on his haunches on the soft mud. He continued smiling. But it was a sad smile. It hurt me no end to disappoint him. But I seemed to be helpless in doing anything about it, no matter how hard I tried.

Then after I had rested for a while, Dattya went to the next round of the exercise regime.

"Let uz run," he said, waiting for me to start. He always gave me a head start. But then invariably, my three surrogate brothers caught up with me. And just as on earlier occasions, I was soon left behind.

My progress on the running and pushups regime was unsatisfactory. Dattya realised that his smiling, coaxing and mild scolding strategies to prod me had failed to push me. Now I needed a big push…rather a big shout and an ultimatum.

Angel Papa, through his miracle, had shed the clumsiness in my legs. That though was only half the battle won. The remaining battle would have to be won by my own efforts. The spring in my step gifted to me by the saint that the Church had banned was just for starters.

Then suddenly I got it! Hallelujah! God be praised! I saw Angel Papa kneeling on the red carpet in front of the village cross, smiling as he prayed, "Our Father…."

It was a vision of the saint, happy in death. A vision sparked by the silence of the woods; the darkness of late evening.

Oh! God, how much my Angel Papa had punished himself while he was alive – collecting the sharpest, most pointed stones to place below his knees, while he prayed past midnight in front of the village Cross, which he was banned from visiting, after his excommunication from the Church. As the cross was close to our home, I often heard him pray, loudly, weeping, pleading, "God forgive me for my sins."

An innocent person is asking forgiveness for sins that the Church cooked up, Daddy would say.

A light sleeper, I used to keep awake recounting the slurs cast on me – on my weakness, my thinness, my clumsiness. So, I could understand the sorrow of a person spurned. Sometimes when Daddy couldn't bear to hear his mentor suffer anymore, he would rush to the cross, and take him home. On some occasions, I would accompany Daddy to the cross.

You love me, Sipee? Angel Papa would ask, weeping.

Yes, Dada, my father would say, holding him by the hand and leading him home.

But then Daddy worked hard and slept soundly. So, he was not always awake to rescue Angel Papa from his misery. Then Baby Mama would arrive at the cross, early morning, to wake up her angel, sleeping near the stones, while villagers queuing up for their water from the public tap, laughed, taunting him, "*Veda manoos.*" (Mad man.)

Now, standing in the dark woods, I waited for Angel Papa to complete the last lines of the Lord's Prayer: *And lead us not into temptation, but deliver us from evil.*

Then I saw his vision fade out, but the smile on his face lingered in my mind. It wouldn't go away. But because of that smile, I got it.

I got the clue to break the jinx to the six-pushups-deadlock.

The crust of the miracle is tough. Go break it, son; you can do it, he seemed to say, smiling.

Then the smile too had gone and I was left to do the hard work on my own.

❤

"…Seven, eight, nine, ten." My face was soaked in mud. Some of the gooey stuff went into my mouth. I spat it out. I was coughing noisily.

My three 'brothers' fell flat on their faces like me, stroking my back.

I was rolling in the mud with joy. They too joined me, rolling about, roaring with laughter.

"Ten pushups, I cannot believing you iz doing," Dada kept saying at least a dozen times. He continued lying in the mud, in no hurry to raise himself. But I must tell you it was really exhilarating to be down there, so close to the wet ground…it felt so calm and soothing.

Mummy wouldn't be so pleased though, it struck me. *How would I explain to her these mud-encrusted clothes?*

At this thought, I jumped from the ground. Dada and my best friends, sorry brothers (you might have noticed dear readers that I have started calling them brothers; that's because they had become more like my family now…extended family of surrogate brothers, one could say) also sprung up after me, laughing.

Dada was laughing the most. He just wouldn't stop laughing. I hadn't seen him laugh like this for almost two months. What a relief to see my hero happy after seeing him smile so sadly, because of my failure to buck up my speed in the exercise regimen.

As I got ready to go home, Dada stopped me, saying, "Wait!"

Now what, I said to myself, and looked up at him, confused. And he was laughing again. "See for your face," he said, laughing.

I obviously couldn't see my face. But I felt it with my fingers, layered with mud. That brought in more mud over my fingers.

"Come, come to my house and washing face," he said, pointing to Hill Mansion on the hillock in the distance.

Anand and Baloo ran up towards their backyard. I chased them and nearly got them as we reached the drum of water outside their hut. Dada didn't run with us, but I could hear his laughter. Perhaps because he had realised that I was suddenly picking up speed in my running too.

A few feet away from their home, my two brothers and I waited for our elder brother. He seemed to be in no hurry, as he was strolling merrily upwards, towards Hill Mansion. When he came up to us, he was smiling happily.

Then I saw Angel Papa again. He wasn't smiling. But he had a sombre, satisfied look on his face. He rose from the red carpet that lay in front of the Cross. He touched his forehead saying, *Glory be to The Father*. Then he touched his heart saying, *The Son*; and touching his left and right shoulders he said, *And to The Holy Spirit*.

Then the saint had gone from the Cross. The red carpet too disappeared.

I closed my eyes to savour the vision, because it seemed like some fine food that was uplifting my spirit. I might have been in this state of bliss for some time, for nothing around seemed to matter anymore, not even the jubilation among my brothers.

When I came around to the real world, it was with a start, for my face was splashed with water and Dada was wiping my face with a towel that smelt stale and musty. But since my face was being cleaned with such tender loving care, the smell and dirt in the towel hardly mattered. After some hard and vigorous rubbing of my face, Dada certified that my face was sparkling new again, as he uttered an ecstatic, "Soh clean and tip top you look, my brother."

And I felt really proud and privileged because Dada had given me first preference and cleaned up Baloo's and Anand's muddy faces after mine. Then Anand took the lead, while Baloo and I joined in cleaning up Dada's face too. He enjoyed the three of us scrubbing him, because he was giggling happily all through the exercise. At the end, the towel was looking like a rag and smelt fouler than when it had first assailed my nostrils. But it was the sharing of that dirty towel to clean our faces that had brought so much of joy to us brothers that we just couldn't stop laughing.

The other occupants of Hill Mansion were, however, not amused at our laughter. Dondya Bhoir, his wife Gangu and their pretty but fiery daughter Shalu were crying foul. "You wasting so lots of water, you damn fools," Shalu screamed, angrily banging her fists on Dada's chest.

He took her blows and continued to laugh. I was stunned as much with her bravery to strike my hero as her use of English that seemed nearly perfect.

Then when Shalu looked at me, her anger evaporated and she smiled so coyly that my heart began to flutter, though by extension she was my sister because she was family after all. But the most pleasant surprise in this unexpected encounter was the father of my foster brothers who appeared as sober as Father Francis to me at that point in time.

"Apan kaun ahot?" (Who are you?) asked Mr Dondya Bhoir, squinting his eyes in the moonlight.

"Arrey, mahit nahi kai, Dattya cha baba, Suplan Saheb cha mulga ahey toh?" (Arrey, don't you know, Dattya's father, he is Suplan Saheb's son?) Gangu bai said.

"Suplan Saheb, cheep engineer cha mulga svata amcha ghari, wah!" (Suplan Saheb, chief engineer's son himself is in our home, great!) he said, grinning. Gangu bai too was grinning widely.

Both husband and wife bore a strange resemblance. Both were reed thin and shrivelled. Both had a good portion of their front teeth missing. In lighter moments, Anand and Baloo had told me about the boxing matches between them. How the children would rush to keep out of reach dangerous objects when the husband and wife got into scrapes, mostly because of Mr Bhoir's drunkenness. The worst consequence of their fights was their broken teeth.

Now it struck me that it was the first time that I had seen the father of my best friends-turned-brothers up and smiling, instead of the usual sight of him sprawled out on the floor.

The pretty Shalu, who was the only sweet smelling person around, because of the mogra flowers that she wore on her long black plaits, broke the suspense of Mr Bhoir's sobriety. "Baba today swearing on Ganapati Deva that he is not going to drink again," she announced cheerily in English, perhaps for my benefit.

My brothers clapped merrily and hugged their father. Shalu joined in the group embrace, while Gangu bai looked on, grinning, front-toothlessly.

I looked on happily, but didn't join the embracing party. When they left each other's embrace, I saw Mr Bhoir look at me wistfully. Although his eyes were beaming with joy, there was a deep trace of sadness hidden inside. On a sudden impulse, I ran up to him and hugged him so tight that I could feel the skin and bones that constituted the frugal mass of his body.

He smelled foul in his dirty clothes and un-bathed body, as he shed buckets of tears that fell all over me. Mr Bhoir still reeked of booze that may have been soaked in his system and breath after many years of consumption. A day of sobriety would not have taken away the ravages of years of drunkenness.

But I didn't mind the smell and squalor at all…because it was one of the finest and purest expressions of love that I had experienced in my twelve years of living.

Thirteen and strong

Saturday, 28th of September, 1963 was when I turned 13 and a certified teenager. There was a big celebration at my home, White House and I cut a huge chocolate cake with shimmering silver white icing.

Daddy took leave to be with me for this special birthday. I was really touched that though Victor didn't have much of a singing voice, he took the lead in singing 'Happy Birthday to you', with Carlton giving the musical score, strumming rhythmically at his box guitar.

The magnificence of the music, however, couldn't rectify the cacophony of the singers, all singing in various unmatched tenors. Victor's valorous croaky singing, Daddy's flat low falsetto tone, my two younger sisters – seven-year-old Debby, and Sandra, aged five – crooning in high pitched voices, made the birthday song sound tuneless. Mummy's dulcet voice, the only one in tune, was drowned in the din. Carlton bravely continued strumming as the family sang, "From old friends and new, many girl friends to you, happy birthday dear Robert, happy birthday to you."

The only member of the family who couldn't join in the singing was my fifteen-month-old baby sister Christine, though now no more a baby-in-arms, but a brisk walker and dancer too. As Daddy did a strange jig, swaying only the left side of his body, hopping only on the left leg, the right side of his body unmoving, Christine hopped along.

Debby and Sandra were graceful dancers and led the dancing after the birthday song was over, as Cartlton and I began singing various popular English and Hindi songs of the times. The non-singers were gracious enough to let us sing.

The favourite English songs were Cliff Richard's 'The Young Ones', the Beatles' 'Love me Do', Elvis Presley's 'Wooden Heart', and Andy Williams' 'The House of Bamboo'. The lead singer in the English songs was Carlton. When it came to Hindi songs, I took the lead for songs like '*Yahoo*' from the Shammi Kapoor-Saira Banu hit movie *Junglee* and '*Ai gulbadan*' from another Shammi film *Professor*. Mummy's favourite Hindi song was '*Tera mera pyar amar*' from the DevAnand-Sadhana blockbuster *Asli Naqli*.

But the hottest favourite by popular demand was Mummy's 'My Love is for a Sailor Boy'.

Daddy looked nostalgic, perhaps thinking of his days as an engineer on the merchant ship. Mummy had pleaded till Daddy gave up his sailor job and took up work in a factory, as she found it difficult to manage the fleet of children on her own. All of us calling together – 'Mummy, listen to what I am saying' – must have been the most cacophonic sound in Golvada village. Mummy was driven crazy and Daddy was needed to find a solution to the chaos. Daddy reciprocated to the Sailor Boy song with the famed Willie Nelson's song – 'With someone like you, a pal good and true' – trying his best to sing in tune.

The solid acknowledgment of my growing up was Daddy's present of exactly thirteen crisp one rupee notes, the biggest amount of cash I had possessed in my life till then at one time.

I merrily pocketed the money, my face lighting up with glee as I shamelessly counted the money to make sure there were thirteen notes when Daddy announced, "Here, son, thirteen rupees for each year of your life on this planet."

Victor had been the first to wish me on my birthday. He was the first to sing happy birthday and it seemed that he would not be satisfied till he proved he was the eldest and the strongest.

So as soon as I placed the money carefully in my pant pocket, he held out his strong right hand and said, "Happy Birthday once more, Robert; may you grow into a strong boy."

I understood what he was getting at. I swallowed my saliva nervously, took a deep breath as if I was about to do a pushup and held his hand.

I watched Victor closely as the smirk on his face turned into a frown and then into a look of utter disbelief.

Ponga Pondya Robert Pereira for the first time in his life didn't feel like his hands were being crushed by elder brother Victor Pereira.

The real birthday bash

Braving the solitude and darkness of the night and the scary screams of wild foxes in the woods nearby, I ran up the small hill on the outskirts of my village Golvada towards the lone ramshackle hut that I loved more than my modern brick, concrete and cement home.

The entrance to Hill Mansion was festooned with buntings and balloons. A small kerosene lamp was shining like a neon light over the tin board, Hill Mansion, that had withstood the vicissitudes of time and the fury of nature, perhaps because it was painted by me out of so much love.

It was almost four years since I had painted that board. But it was the first time that I had seen it shine so magnificently, because it was the first time that I had ventured into their deserted home at night.

Buntings and balloons were strewn across the bamboo walls of the hut and the cow dung flooring was decorated with an array of coloured powder or gulal used during the Holi festival. The Bhoirs, my extended family, had acquired a second-hand folding table that was already falling apart, and some seven-odd chairs that seemed to have come straight out of the junk yard. On the table was spread an assortment of snacks that included *bhajias* or *pakodas, batata vadas, farsan, gulab jamuns* as well as plastic bottles full of red sherbet.

As soon as I entered Hill Mansion, Anand, Baloo and Dattya, jumped up from the floor, clapping and whistling to welcome me, shouting together, "*Vadh divasachya subbhechha*, Robert!" (Happy Birthday, Robert!)

A smiling, sober Mr Dondya Bhoir waited patiently for his sons to finish hugging me, after which he gave me a gentle embrace. He smelled of fresh talcum powder.

His wife, Gangu bai was in the corner of the room, frying a fresh lot of bhajiyas. She got up from the floor, grinning widely. She placed both her hands on my head, blessing me, and then pressed her knuckles on her temples and cracked them, apparently to ward off any evil that might come my way.

I was so overjoyed with my second birthday celebration that I didn't notice that Shalu wasn't around. She soon announced her arrival to the beating of a dholak, emerging from the darkness of the backyard of Hill Mansion.

My heart was fluttering more than ever when I saw her prance around in a bright red new sari, her hair covered with not the usual small string of mogra flowers on the plait of her hair, but a big bunch over the crown of her hair, falling across her temples.

"Happy Birthday to you, my younger brother," she piped in a high pitch, raising her voice over her own loud beating of the drum.

I was clean bowled or rather stumped by both her flawless English and her vivacity. The fact that she had called me younger brother, being three years older than me and being a part of my extended family, didn't stop the strange emotions building up inside me.

Then she stopped beating the drum and lay it down on the floor. She ruffled my hair, the way my hero Dattya did, and then gave me a gentle hug.

Her three brothers, father and mother clapped. Dattya lifted the drum from the floor and started beating it. The applause and sound of the drum failed to drown the impulses within me and I was struggling to control the surge of feelings for her.

So, when Dattya Dada announced, "Now iz birthday party going start, but first all my three brothers going to do show," I was relieved.

On a cue from Dada, Anand, Baloo and I were on all fours on the floor. Dada shouted, "Start" and we began.

"One, two, three, four, five, six, seven, eight, nine, ten, eleven, twelve, thirteen, fourteen, fifteen, sixteen," Dada counted as the three of us went up and down in a slow, rhythmic movement. He stopped the count and beat the drum loudly. I felt like my chest and arms were made of steel, after the neatly done sixteen pushups. When the drumming of the dholak had ceased, there was a round of applause.

Anand, Baloo and I bowed like artistes from a circus. Then Dada led the birthday party to the backyard. There were two three-fourths full buckets of water tied to a wooden pole.

"Robert, you iz first doing, ten times," Dada commanded.

I lifted the buckets, like I was lifting weights on a crossbar in the gymnasium. Dattya counted from one to ten. When I had completed ten, I gingerly placed the contraption down, so as to not spill any water. Anand and Baloo lifted the buckets on the pole, with greater aplomb, I thought.

The next demonstration was on parallel bars that Dada had got prefabricated in a workshop and dug deep into the ground in the backyard. I did a dozen pull-ups and so did my two brothers. Dattya had carried the dholak outside and went for another loud round of drum beating. In the darkness, I could see Shalu's lovely smile at her brother's celebratory drumming. That smile sent my heart soaring once again.

Then as we feasted on the snacks and sherbet, with me given the honour of sitting at the head of the table, I couldn't take my eyes off Shalu. She smiled at me but I couldn't detect any reciprocation of the feelings that I felt for her. I guessed she didn't have a clue about what was going on inside my heart.

Surrounded by so much of pure love around me, despite my impure thoughts for her, I gorged on the snacks and drank a couple of glasses of the sherbet. Dada had arranged for plenty of paper plates, plastic glasses, and even tissue paper for my birthday celebrations.

When the table was swept clean of the snacks and the sherbet bottles were empty, I decided it was time to go and got up from my seat of honour. I had sneaked out of the house, without informing Mummy or Daddy, afraid that if I told them where I was going at that late hour, they would stop me. I estimated it would be about 10.00 p.m. With the exercise demos and the big feast, the celebrations had lasted longer than I had anticipated.

"Wait, wait," Dattya said, as he saw that I was about to leave. The whole Bhoir family now were standing near me, smiling.

Now what is the next pleasant surprise, I wondered.

It was not just a pleasant surprise; it was a bonanza. I couldn't accept it from Dada, because he was being too generous. "No Dada, thirteen rupees is too much. I can't accept," I said emphatically as he counted thirteen crisp notes like Daddy had and handed them over to me.

Shalu strode up to me, hands on the side of her hips. "Younger brother, we are poor but our hearts are rich, ha," she said, pouting. Oh my God, what was I going to do with my heart now! It wouldn't stop pounding at the sight of Shalu.

I looked at Dada. He seemed to be wiping a tear off his left eye. Was it a tear of joy or sorrow? I couldn't tell. But that did it. I couldn't bear to see that tear. I pocketed the money.

They all hugged me, one by one, including Gangu bai.

That was one of the happiest nights of my life.

The next morning I got up with a pleasant sensation. I had dreamt about Shalu.

But I was ashamed of myself and prayed to God for forgiveness.

Teen troubles

How many times does God forgive us? Seventy times seven was what my saintly Father Francis had said, quoting the Gospel. But as I turned thirteen and my puberty seemed to be bursting out of my pants virtually, I began to silently question Father Francis' teachings in the disturbed corners of my mind.

I feel embarrassed saying this, but I must confess that my self-induced ejaculations were becoming frequent and gave me great pleasure, making me feel grown up and wonder why those many enjoyable acts were that many sins. I was alarmed that if each of these acts were counted as sins, I would soon exhaust the seventy times seven forgiveness quota.

Purity of thought, word and deed sounded good in my innocent preteen years, but now it was becoming difficult to observe and the heavy burden of sin was playing havoc with my peace of mind. I fell deeper into sin, as I also began to question Father Francis' teachings.

All these years, I believed what Father Francis told us in Catechism class – "God blesses those who are poor and realise their need for him, for the Kingdom of Heaven is theirs."

I had believed Father Francis because it meant that my poor friends Anand and Baloo and my hero Dattya, now my extended family, were assured of a place in Heaven. I was so blind in my faith that I even imagined that they being poor would overrule the condition that the only way to Heaven is through Christ.

I can still recall the many times in my preteen days when I would go down on my knees in front of the altar in our living room in White House in the middle of the night when everyone was fast asleep and with tears in my eyes pray to Jesus Christ on the cross, pleading that he allow Anand, Baloo and Dattya entry into Heaven. But now would God listen to my prayers, since I had sinned so much? If I myself was in danger of burning in the fires of Hell, how could I save my friends, my adopted brothers, whom I loved more than my own brothers?

But was it really my fault? Was I to blame if I had suddenly begun to feel pleasure in playing with myself? Why was it a sin? I was thoroughly confused. I just couldn't understand!

I was no longer weak physically. But my soul seemed to be getting weaker. I was no longer spiritually strong.

Then on Friday, the 31st of May, 1964, the pre-stamped, self-addressed envelope containing my eighth standard results contained two shockers.

First, my rank in class had dropped from the usual second or third to tenth. Second, there was no chit in the envelope asking me to collect my prize for scoring the highest in religion, as had been happening since the first standard.

Tragedy strikes
Hill Mansion

❦

When Mummy opened the envelope containing my results, her nostrils flared with anger and her eyes turned very big and red. She opened her mouth to yell at me, but she seemed too stunned to speak. Daddy used to always call Mummy, 'My pretty Moonie'. But Mummy's pretty face was now an ugly, scary scowl.

My first reaction was to run away. So I tried to bolt away from her. Mummy had lost her speech in her anger, but her reflexes were still fast. She pounced on me, held me firmly with her left hand, and flung away the result that she held in her right hand…slapping me hard across my right cheek.

The slap really stung. It was the hardest slap of my life. But I didn't cry and bravely held back my tears. I think Mummy thought that my not shedding any tears was as an act of defiance. She struck me again on the same stinging spot, it seemed with deliberate precision.

Yes, I was defiant. I didn't move and stood with my hands on my waist, waiting for Mummy to strike me again. She did and much harder this time and on the same burning right cheek, on exactly the same spot.

Then Mummy slapped me the fourth time, as I continued challenging her authority by standing defiantly in front of her. But a Mummy is a mother and she soon broke down, sobbing.

I was probably what parents call a stonehearted boy, because Mummy's tears didn't move me. On the contrary, deep down I felt that she was paying the price for punishing me so much for going down in my rank in class and not scoring the highest marks in religion, which was anyway not counted in the total.

As Mummy sank into a chair in the living room and continued sobbing, I made no move to console her or promise her that I would do better in the coming academic year.

I had been on the lookout for the postman for the past few days, near the main road outside our village. As soon as I had seen him trudging in his khaki uniform with his khaki-coloured big bag full of letters, I stopped him and asked, "Postman sir, do you have a letter for Robert Pereira, White House, 146, Golvada, Thana?"

He had smiled benevolently, because he knew it was my result that I had been waiting for. Searching in his bag, he had handed over the envelope. Like a good son, I had handed over the envelope to my mother so that she would be the first to see the good news.

I had never imagined that I would be carrying home bad news – of my worst ever examination results.

Then, my bad news sounded really tragic when Victor rushed in, screaming, "Mummy, I stood first in class."

Mummy was still so stunned by my results that it took her a while to react to Victor's big news. It took some effort for Mummy to get up from the chair where she was sitting slouched in sorrow and congratulate Victor. However, instead of laughing with joy at Victor's topmost rank, Mummy began sobbing.

"Mummy, are you not happy with my first rank?" Victor asked, looking bewildered.

"I am very happy, son," she said, sobbing.

"Then why are you crying, Mummy?" he asked.

Oh, no! I was wishing that Mummy wouldn't tell Victor the reason for her tears, because I dreaded that Victor would laugh at me when he learnt that I had plummeted in my rank.

But I was surprised at Victor's reaction to Mummy's disclosure, "I am not crying for you, but because your younger brother has gone down to number ten in class."

I couldn't believe my eyes. Victor looked genuinely concerned, even sad.

He first consoled Mummy, tenderly wiping the tears trickling down her cheeks. Then, he came up to me, patted me on my back affectionately and said, "Don't worry Robert, you'll get back your rank and even do better next year."

I didn't know what to make of Victor's kindness and how to react to his show of affection. To be honest, I suspected that he was just showing off his first rank and pretending to be kind, because it made him feel superior.

However, after Victor's announcement of his first rank and his consolatory words to me, Mummy seemed pacified. She picked up my result that she had flung away and put it back in the envelope. Then as Victor handed over his result to her to see, she was all smiles.

Coming up to me, she lovingly rubbed my right cheek, which I thought was still sore, and said tenderly, "Promise, you'll do better next year!"

"I promise," I said, trying to sound as sincere as I could, given that I was still resentful of the rain of slaps that I had received from Mummy.

"I'll help you, if you have any difficulties," Victor said, sounding so magnanimous.

That was the last thing I would accept – help from Victor. His help always came with a hook. He had no patience and would strike you if you were not quick in learning and called you 'duffer' each time you made a mistake. So, I nodded unenthusiastically to Victor's offer.

God, if only Dattya Dada was educated. He is such an excellent teacher, I brooded. *It didn't matter really if he wasn't educated; he always gave sound advice*, I thought.

So, as Mummy got busy in the kitchen, I sneaked out from home to go to Hill Mansion – my retreat of love and solace.

My clumsiness was now a distant memory, and I glided up the hillock to Hill Mansion, my heart beating with excitement each time I entered my haven. But I was greeted inside with a roar of sorrow.

Mr Bhoir was sitting on his haunches, reeking of alcohol and sobbing like he was in the throes of a convulsion. Gangu bai had buried her head into his chest and was wailing.

My hero Dattya Dada was beating his chest endlessly, his long hair matted and wet with sweat and tears. Anand and Baloo were bawling like infants in two different corners of the hut.

I didn't know what to do. Whom should I console first?

As I looked from one distraught face to the other, I realised that they were so immersed in their sorrow that none of them had even noticed my arrival. Gathering courage, I dived to the ground and held Dattya Dada's face with both my hands. Dattya buried his head in my chest and sobbed violently.

"What happened, Dada?" I had to yell over Dattya's wailing to be heard.

"Your sister Shalu is running away to sell the body to peoples," he blurted out.

"What?" I asked.

"She iz not good girl," he said, taking his head away from my chest, beating his own so hard and incessantly that I was afraid he would break his rib cage.

"My *daakta bahu* (younger brother) you iz too *bhola* (innocent); you iz not understanding all diz dirty things," he said.

But I was grown up enough to understand.

I was sobbing, wracked by guilt that I myself had been consumed by desire for Shalu.

My first kiss

It's a difficult choice for me to make! Which was the best day of my life so far: Sunday, the 4th of June, 1961, when I played my first cricket match and scored the winning stroke, or Friday the 25th of December, 1965? At age eleven, I would have cast my 'best day' vote for the winning stroke. But at the grown up boy age of fifteen years and almost three months, I am blindly voting for the early hours of Christmas in 1965 as the best day of my life.

'Blindly Voting' is the most appropriate phrase because it was with closed eyes that I kissed Rachael Dias standing around the Christmas bonfire in front of the over century-old banyan tree. So far, I had seen kisses only in English movies, which would always evoke pleasant quivering sensations down my shorts and a wish that I should have been in the place of that lucky guy on the screen. But those lucky guys always had their eyes open before the kisses and closed them only later when they got into the thick of things.

But I found the adrenaline rush so strong and gushing that I closed my eyes as soon as I held her silky tender face in my hands and gently drew her close to me. Then like in the English movies, our lips brushed against each other. But unlike the movies, our kiss ended quickly, in just a few seconds.

Rachael's lips felt so soft…softer than they looked in the light of the bonfire, before I had closed my eyes. I didn't open my eyes for some time – both to savour the kiss and to avoid looking at others around the bonfire.

Although nicknamed the 'tomboy' of our village Golvada, Rachael was extremely pretty with cat-like grey eyes. She earned the nickname tomboy because she roamed around barefoot, abusing and even boxing boys who dared to tease her.

She was not an invitee to the all-boys' Christmas party that began around 2 a.m. after we had all attended the midnight mass in St John the Evangelist Church. But the daredevil that she was, she barged into our party.

Ignoring her scores of admirers, she singled me out among all the boys around the bonfire and wished me 'Merry Christmas' with a handshake that seemed too soft for a tomboy.

She wouldn't let go my hand and soon held both my hands, looking soulfully into my eyes. After a couple of minutes, she gradually released my hands, but continued looking at me and came so close to me that I could feel her breath – so warm in a cold winter night. Then it seemed so natural for me to hold her soft face and close my eyes. Her lips brushed against mine, and we kissed for a few seconds. I don't know if this is what is described as bliss, but it was definitely the best few seconds of my life so far.

Rachael had been scouring the dark unlit village, accompanied by her five-year-old brother, who was wearing a Santa cap and blowing a long plastic whistle like it were a trumpet to announce Christmas. During our kiss, Rachael's kid brother stopped blowing his 'trumpet'. But as soon as the kiss ended, he resumed playing it.

There was a strange silence as the boys seemed overwhelmed by her sudden appearance. She looked stunning in a pink silk dress, wearing high-heeled shoes, probably the first time that we had seen her with footwear. After the kiss, Rachael left without a word, sprinting away, her high heels making sharp clicking sounds in the silent night. As she disappeared inside the village lanes, the boys around the bonfire suddenly found their voices.

"So cheap, to come and kiss a boy in front of the whole world," I heard Victor shout.

Milton Aguiar whom Rachael had once boxed for making a pass at her said, "She is a *chalu* girl."

Clarence D'Silva, who continued to be my thick friend, shouted at Milton, "You are just jealous, you bugger." Coming up to me, Clarence handed over a glass of hot coffee that was being made in a kettle on a makeshift fireplace and said, "Robert, you are a lucky guy."

The basket containing pieces of plum cake was passed around. As I bit into a piece, I couldn't help saying to myself, *She is sweeter than this cake.* I closed my eyes and saw her standing in front of me, smiling with her full soft lips. I imagined that she was back, kissing me again. I was woken from my fantasy by Clarence's melodious voice singing the hit song *'Yun to humne lakh haseen dekhe hein'* from the Bollywood movie, *Tumsa Nahi Dekha.*

The pleasant sensations that the singing sent through my brain heightened my vision of Rachael and brought memories of our encounter some eight months ago, during 'Our Lady Of Hope' festival celebrations. As I had sat brooding after the festival mass in a lonely broken down archway of Our Lady of Hope Church, she had sneaked up towards me, startling me with a loud, "Hey hero, why are you looking so sad and lonely?"

Here I was, face-to-face with my dream girl around whom I had built countless fantasies, her dazzling grey eyes looking at me with concern. In my fantasies, I would say so many smart words to her, as I pictured myself with muscles rippling out of my shirt sleeves, the puff of my hair a perfect shape in the style of my superhero, Dev Anand.

But I was at a total loss for words and looked down at my shoes when I really saw her standing in front of me. Rachael held out her hand, saying, "Robert, I promise, that from today, you will never be sad."

I had never held a girl's hand before. When I held hers, it sent a pleasant, tingling sensation down my entire body. Her offer to take away my sadness forever had bowled me clean over. But during the eight months after the handshake, there had not been much interaction. When we bumped into each other in our village, our conversation never went beyond a 'Hi, how are you?'

Despite my growing muscles, I was still a shy boy. Rachael too turned coy when we came across each other. But being braver than me, she had made the first bold move on Christmas.

My first kiss and most likely, even hers, was sure to change our relationship and our lives.

From Ponga Pondya
to He-Man

My life did change as Rachael and I got closer and cosier. She was no more a dream but a reality. So, I had to stop fantasising and prove myself to her by action. I was dying to impress her and make sure that she stayed my girlfriend. There were so many boys in our village still vying for her attention, especially Milton who had not given up on her and said that her insults to him really hid the love that she felt for him.

Two years older than me, Milton bought new clothes to get her attention and had started going to the gym to build his muscles. Milton's family was loaded with cash. But money was in short supply in our home. My father's designation of chief engineer didn't come with a fat salary, provoking my mother to call him in jest, 'cheap engineer'.

There was no way that Daddy would spare money for the gym, considering that with the addition of one more brother to our family a year ago, we were now seven children to feed and clothe, plus school fees for five. With the youngest baby sister Christine almost three years old, scheduled to join junior KG the next year, the school-going children would increase to six.

We all had ravenous appetites and as we were growing up, we quickly outgrew our clothes. The Pereira progeny had all immense king-size egos and the younger children never wore the old clothes of the older siblings. Daddy had no choice but to control spending strictly. Any unnecessary request for money was met with a vehement refusal by Daddy, who had developed a stock reply, "What for you want money, forget it!"

My top priority was to get stronger and build real big muscles to ensure that no boy stole Rachael from me. Would I be able to do it without going to the gym and lifting weights to build muscles was the question that worried me no end. Rachael and I had frequent rendezvous in cosy corners on the outskirts of Golvada, our hotspot being the shade and secrecy amidst a cluster of tamarind trees at the village's west end.

On one occasion, Rachael held my arm and said, "You have nice muscles, but I want you to build stronger muscles, man!"

"I do thirty pushups at a stretch every day," I had boasted, adding an extra ten to my actual tally.

"You should do ten more, then," she had said. "I want my boyfriend to be a real he-man." I knew forty pushups were impossible for me, as it would mean doubling my count.

One day, Rachael suddenly challenged me to beat her in speed in climbing the topmost branch of the tallest tamarind tree. And before I could say Jack Robinson, she had scaled up the tree. The way she expertly dug her bare feet into the bark of the tree to facilitate her climb, it seemed like she had been doing this regularly. When I joined her on top of the tree, after several minutes, she laughed and said, "You know I made a big mistake in making a slow coach my boyfriend and kissing him."

She looked pretty and the pout of her lips that often challenged and abused boys, looked soft and attractive like the petals of a red rose. We both seemed to have involuntarily inched closer to each other on the tamarind tree. I brushed my lips against hers. She allowed me to kiss her for just a few seconds, after which she pushed my face away.

"Don't kiss me too much or I'll get pregnant," she said, her voice full of alarm.

Now it was my turn to laugh. "Why are you laughing?" she asked, sounding miffed. I didn't answer her but continued laughing.

"I may not be so lucky this time, though I escaped the first time when we kissed on Christmas," she said. This was our second kiss in two months. I was disappointed that it had ended as quickly as the first. But now I understood that the reason for her abrupt ending of the kiss was her funny fear that she would get pregnant.

"Rachael, you can never get pregnant by kissing," I said, affectionately rubbing her soft silken face with my hands.

"Of course you do, Robert, if you kiss too much," she insisted. "That is why married women and those girls who have had boyfriends for a long time get pregnant," she added, moving away from me on the tamarind tree.

"Rachael, you only get pregnant if you do that without your clothes," I explained to her.

I might have sounded really vague, for Rachael's face looked clouded with confusion. "Do that? Do what?" she asked imperiously.

I had imagined countless times the 'that' that I was referring to. But there was no way I could have explained the act to her, especially since she was invariably the subject of my fantasy. Now as I saw her moving further away from me on the tamarind tree, I felt sad. Then just as she had quickly climbed to the top of the tree, she slithered down in barely a minute. I descended slowly after her. She was patiently waiting for me at the trunk of the tree.

While I gathered my breath, she said, softly, "Robert, prove to me that you love me by pasting Milton." I wasn't sure if I would be able to bash him up, but I nodded my head.

"Robert, he keeps making passes at me and saying why are you going after Ponga Pondya Robert, when I am there, richer and stronger," she said and scraped her teeth angrily, making her look very pretty, I thought.

"I'll hammer him till he begs for mercy," I heard myself saying.

Rachael pulled my face towards hers by tugging at my hair. As I screamed "Ouch," she kissed me on my lips for a second and threw my head back.

"You are my he-man, my hero," she said and darted into the village.

Hill Mansion was
my church

I was in deep trouble. I should have gone to Church and prayed to God to give me the strength to get me out of trouble. But I knew that knocking on the doors of the Church would not help me.

Stronger I was growing by the day, but was I strong enough to 'paste' Milton as ordered by Rachael?

I was still mortally afraid of coming to blows with boys. I had seen Milton beat the hell out of boys who interfered with him in school and in our village. Though of lean built, he was firm and muscular, with mean, thin lips that would twist in a wicked smile when he smelt victory.

My generous full lips that Rachael so loved to kiss crinkled with despondency at the thought of the tough opponent that I was up against and I repeatedly bit both my upper and lower lip in desperation.

"Oh Jesus!" I exclaimed. But I knew that Jesus, my God, whom I had often prayed to as a kid was not the saviour who could save me. In my boyhood I was becoming distant from my God and more cynical but realistic by the day.

The Church and God were of no use to a fast-growing boy like me, who after serious sins of the flesh, first in thought, then in deed, was now entering the realm of hatred and violence.

So many times as a kid, I had prayed to God to send His guardian angels to protect me from the strong, bad boys…and to give me wings like his angels in Heaven so that I could fly, instead of dragging my legs clumsily and inviting ridicule and earning the nickname Pondya, and then a double whammy Ponga Pondya tag.

I would go to Church before the Mass started or stay back after it ended to pray to God, as I believed He would hear me better in His House. In Church, I felt I was so close to God.

But the Church was only a nice, peaceful place to console my broken heart and shattered spirit. My closeness to God was of no help in dealing with the strong boys or my big bully brother Victor.

Dattya Dada and my best friends Anand and Baloo, brothers really, were the ones who were helping me to grow strong. I believed that Angel Papa, whom the Church had thrown out of its fold, and not God's angels, had given wings to my legs.

So, dear reader, please don't think I am being blasphemous when I say that Hill Mansion was my church and Dattya Dada was like my god.

And it was to Hill Mansion that my legs carried me to help me get out of the deep trouble that I seemed to have gotten myself into, after Rachael's command that I 'paste' Milton to retain her friendship…the friendship that came with nice, sweet kisses.

▼

Hill Mansion seemed less crowded and even more spacious. The size of the family was truncated from six members to four. Shalu who had run away from home never returned, despite Dattya Dada tracing her living in a house of ill-repute and begging her to return. Seized by sorrow, their father had resumed his drinking and died of cirrhosis of the liver.

But my extended family bounced back to life. The lady of the house, Gangu bai, whom I now called Aai (mother) washed utensils and clothes in lesser number of homes, for Dattya earned more money as he was now a skilled carpenter and Anand and Baloo worked as his helpers.

My entry into Hill Mansion had always been like a whirlwind ever since Angel Papa blessed me with wings to my legs and Dattya Dada had helped me to not only multiply that speed but also to build muscle power in my arms.

However, Rachael's command took the wind out of my sails. So, while I entered Hill Mansion to a tumultuous welcome, I virtually staggered inside, weighed down by worry and despondency.

"What iz happening to you, younger brother?" asked Dattya Dada, as I slouched into one of the unpolished, non-cushioned wooden chairs.

The carpenter Bhoir family had now made chairs for themselves, though they had not indulged in the luxury of upholstery and polish. I was slouching on a chair rather clumsily with my chin almost touching the tip of my chest.

Dattya Dada was really god, for he sensed that I was in trouble. He got up from his seat, came up to me, and ruffled my hair. That gave an instant boost to my spirit.

He hauled me up from the chair with the great power in his hands, standing me up and then pinning my feet to the ground by pressing my shoulders with the immense force of his calloused hands. It seemed like I was affixed to the floor and no matter how much I tried to wriggle out of his grip, I failed to move even an inch.

"You coming to our house after long, long time; so I now fixing you to the floor here," Dada said, grinning.

My visits to Hill Mansion had become less frequent and of shorter duration ever since Rachael came into my life, because meeting her every day for at least an hour or two stole away the time for my visits to my extended family.

They never ever complained and understood, because they loved me too much to demand time and attention. They knew all about my relationship with Rachael, but they maintained a discreet silence about it.

As Dada released his grip and gave me a warm bear hug, with Anand and Baloo joining in, I heard Aai cry with delight.

The three brothers were really celebrating the homecoming of their brother and wouldn't let go of their embrace.

I didn't have to tell my brothers the reason for my visit or the cause for my worry. Dada, Anand and Baloo had all sensed it. So, I was not surprised when Dada said matter-of-factly, "Now I teach you how iz to fighting your enemies like *veda bael* (a mad bull)."

And then Dada started my training. Releasing me from the circle of embrace with the three of them, Dada twirled me around and threw me down on the cow dung floor. I sprung up and charged at Dada like a raging bull, butting him in the stomach with my head.

Dada fell to the ground in a heap. Aai was clapping her hands with delight. Anand and Baloo ran up to me and took turns in shaking hands with me. The head butt was a little too real, for Dada was moaning, rubbing his belly and groaning, *"Aai ga."*

As he grinned, nodding approvingly at me, I went up to him and gave him a hand, so that he could hoist himself from the floor. One hand was not enough to lift him. So, I offered him both my hands. He came up from the floor and kept ruffling my hair for a few minutes.

It seemed that Dada was ruffling my hair for an unusually long time, not only out of affection, but also to tease me a bit. I could figure out that the Dev Anand puff that I had made with extra care that evening – dabbing it with Brylcreem so that it didn't get spoilt in the breeze of the tamarind tree, during my date with Rachael – would have been upset.

Dada seemed to have read my mind, as he said, "Now you looking like fighter hero Shammi Kapoor and not like loving hero Dev Anand." The comparison between the two actors was not lost on me. My illiterate Dada was indeed a good teacher, for he knew how to drive home a point.

"Come now you iz doing thirty pushups," he ordered, pushing me roughly away.

Dada was bull-baiting me, for he had a wicked smile on his face. And how did he come up with the figure of thirty pushups, exactly the same number that I had lied about to Rachael?

"Come he-man, doing thirty pushups," Dada said.

He-man? Was there some sort of telepathy between Dada and Rachael? I wondered.

I went down with my hands on the cow dung floor and fell flat on my face after doing twenty-five pushups. I didn't know Aai could let out a shrill whistle by inserting her thumb and forefinger into her mouth, just like roadside heroes. She did it, not once but thrice in succession to the glee of her sons, who then, imitating their Aai didn't stop whistling for several minutes.

Then Dattya went to the backyard and returned with a stout, heavy club, thin at one end and thick at the other that I had seen him swing around his back and front to build muscle. He demonstrated how to use it, both with his left and right hands a number of times. I could barely manage to do the exercise a couple of times with both hands. But my attempts were greeted with a round of whistles led by Aai. With so much love and applause from my extended family, I was no longer afraid of fighting Milton Aguiar.

Counting my blessings

Two months of rigorous training in fighting like a mad bull gave me bruises and bumps, but Dattya Dada wouldn't budge from the punishing routine. The fights were not mock, but almost real. Though Dada took the knocks from me, laughing, and volunteered to become target practice, sometimes he threw in a real punch or a cross-legged kick across my ankles that sent me rattling down on the floor…just to demonstrate the weaknesses of my assault.

Dada was my sparring partner, but Anand and Baloo were put up against me as 'real' opponents to gauge the progress of my fighting skills. Even though they restrained themselves and didn't fight back with full force, I was beaten hollow by them. Quite clearly, I had a long way to go. So Dada enhanced the rigour of my exercises to toughen me and make me a raging bull, not just in name, but in reality too.

The pushups were increased to two sets of thirty each and I was made to do hundreds of squats. The pull-ups on the parallel bars in the backyard of Hill Mansion were also increased to fifteen at a stretch in two sets. I was made to swing the wooden club without counting, till I broke down out of sheer exhaustion. Then I would plead with Dada to reduce the rigour as Milton was not so strong that I should train like I was competing for a national bout. But Dada would not relent and said that he was training me to fight even the worst of goons.

He said as an elder brother it was his duty to make me so strong that nobody would have the courage to ever call me names.

"I believes in loves and *shanti* (peace)," Dada would say. "But I don't believes that anyone can calls for you bad names."

Dattya Dada, Anand and Baloo had never ever called me the derogatory Ponga Pondya even while referring to the term. They were so sensitive to my feelings that they would euphemistically term it 'bad names'.

My faith in God was dwindling as I was growing up. But my belief in Him would return like a gushing spring when I thought how He had blessed me with the love of Dattya, Anand and Baloo. I shed tears of joy whenever I counted them as the three blessings in my life.

I also thanked God for my fourth blessing and the love of my life – Rachael. I believed that she had laid down the condition that I 'paste' Milton more for my own good than to get him off her back…to prove to the world that I was not a clumsy weakling and could defend the honour of my girlfriend.

However, I hid the identity of my training coach from Rachael, as Dattya Dada, Anand and Baloo advised me against revealing it, because they thought that would take away the credit from me. Their advice further proved how pure and selfless their love really was.

The big fight

Though my thick friend Clarence D'Silva had dropped out from school, he was a great organiser and a boy with brilliant ideas as well as a mind full of drama. He suggested that I challenge Milton Aguiar to fight in the open and promised to gather an audience to witness the bout. Clarence even collected money from the boys of our village, with me giving the largest contribution of five rupees, to build a fighting ring. He volunteered to convey my challenge to Milton and also be the referee.

The fighting ring was facing Golvada's ancient banyan tree. The ring was a square, fifteen by fifteen feet arena, carved out of a maidan that the villagers used for public events. The maidan was uneven, but Clarence with the help of a few village boys had levelled up the ring and patted it down with red mud. Bamboo poles were implanted firmly in the ground. Ropes had been fastened to the poles and across the ring, leaving a small entrance for the contestants and the referee.

My elder brother Victor, who was on vacation from St Xavier's College, Bombay, escorted me to the ring, promising that he would keep the 'secret' of my fight and not tattle to Mummy. Daddy was at work and Mummy was busy in the kitchen.

To ensure that our younger brother Carlton kept his mouth shut, Victor gave him a bribe of three rupees, which was one-fourth of his pocket money for the week. Ever since he joined college and had acquired a few girlfriends, Victor seemed to have become less of a bully and sometimes even condescendingly said that I was looking 'a bit strong these days'.

I thanked God silently and him loudly when he said, "Robert brother, you are going to win this fight, because your elder brother is blessing you."

A tear trickled down my right eye. But I quickly wiped it away, because this was not a day for tears. It was one of the most important days of the fifteen years and seven months of my life. The day – Thursday, the 28th of April 1966 – has been etched in my memory forever, because it was the day of the big fight with Milton.

When Victor and I arrived at the fighting ring with Carlton in tow, there was already an audience, consisting mostly of boys and girls. A few retired old men looked around with curiosity. But being a weekday, the younger men were at work.

Clarence was standing in the centre of the ring and waved out to me, blowing his shrill-sounding referee whistle. He then put the whistle aside and grinned, looking somewhere behind me. I turned around to see Rachael with her younger brother and her two younger sisters running towards the ring, as if they were in a tearing hurry.

Rachael was dressed for the occasion, wearing a pink silk dress and white high-heeled shoes. I recalled it was the same Christmas attire that she had worn on the 25th of December 1965, the first time we had kissed. And as the rays of the sun fell on her pretty face and she squinted to keep away the light from her grey eyes, I noticed that she had a touch of bright pink lipstick that highlighted the pout of her lips.

I closed my eyes, dreaming of those lips. But I was rudely woken up by the beating of drums and loud whistles.

Milton had arrived, flanked by his two elder brothers, who ran a fairly successful transport company. Ahead of them was a cheering party of half a dozen men, three of them with bongos strung with strings around their necks. The bongo men were beating the drums forcefully and their companions were whistling loudly but tunelessly.

Their arrival at the fighting venue drew an instant reaction from Rachael. Standing at some distance from me so far, she ran towards me and clung to my arm.

Getting on top of the din of the Milton party, she shouted in my ear, "Robert my hero, my he-man, you are going to win this fight."

I turned around and looked into her eyes that were so full of love and concern.

I'll fight a thousand battles for you, I was going to tell her.

But I didn't get a chance to tell her so, because I was distracted by Clarence, who was blowing his whistle in one loud, long hoot, rushing from the centre of the ring towards the Milton party at breakneck speed.

"Milton, I will not allow drums to be played around this ring," he shouted.

"Yes, yes, this will distract the contestants," Victor chipped in.

"I don't think I'll get distracted; then why should he...," Milton said, muttering his last words, under his breath.

From Milton's lip movements, I knew what those words were – Ponga Pondya for sure.

Then the attention of the entire audience that had been building up with speed, turned towards the beating of three dholaks; and a loud, continuous whistle that grew into a crescendo as the party approached the fighting ring.

The Bhoir brothers – Dattya, Anand and Baloo – were all three wearing brand new white trousers, starched white shirts, and white canvas shoes, their foreheads dabbed with red tilaks. A whistling Gangu Aai was donning a red sari and matching red sandals.

Dattya, Anand and Baloo circled me and began beating their dholaks.

When Clarence blew his whistle, shaking his head disapprovingly, the Bhoir brothers drowned the sound by banging louder on their dholaks. But, unlike the Milton party, there was a great rhythm to the beating of the dholaks. The Milton Bongo party tried to compete with the Bhoir brothers, but their beat sounded hollow and weak in comparison.

Clarence now altered the rules of the fight and shouted at the top of his voice, "Okay, drums and dholaks are allowed."

He held Milton by the hand and took him into the ring. As Milton, wearing black track pants and a grey tee shirt, puffed up his firm athletic chest, clicking the heels of his gleaming sneakers, Clarence ran his fingers over him from tip to toe, to check whether he was concealing any weapon in his person.

Satisfied that Milton was clean, Clarence walked out of the ring, came up to me standing on the periphery and led me to where Milton was. To appear fair, he ran his fingers over me as well. I was wearing sports shorts and old shoes that I wore for PT in school. I might have looked inferior in dress in comparison to Milton, for I could see him study me from tip to toe and laugh openly at me.

The referee now stood in between the two of us and held up both our hands and then pushed us away a little distance from each other. Retreating many paces backwards, the referee blew his whistle and shouted, "Start fighting Milton and Robert!"

His hands on the side of his hips, Milton walked casually but cockily towards me and shouted, "Ponga Pondya, run for your life or I'll beat the shit out of you."

"Robert, paste the bastard," I could hear Rachael shout.

"Go, go run home, Ponga Pondya!" Milton said, coming close and looking menacingly at me, twisting the two sides of his thin, but growing moustache.

I stared at him. He grinned and again opened his mouth to speak. I could see the words Ponga Pondya forming on his lips again.

I ran many paces backwards almost to the edge of the ring, as he continued standing in the centre, laughing aloud.

Then I ran back towards him at full speed and butted him in the pit of his stomach.

He fell to the ground like he was a sack of cement thrown at a construction site.

As he moaned with pain, I jumped on him, locked his neck with my left hand, and with my right hand, 'pasted' him on his face, mercilessly.

Dhaab, dhaab. I heard the dull sounds of his flesh as I punched his face.

He was struggling to free himself from my grip, kicking up his legs and throwing aimless punches at me. But I wouldn't stop my incessant assault.

After a few minutes, he stopped struggling and lay there, taking the 'pasting' quietly, yelling with pain when a punch hit him too hard.

Then Clarence rushed towards us and started counting, "One, two, three, four, five, six, seven, eight, nine and ten."

I had stopped punching Milton before Clarence had finished counting ten, as Milton now made no effort to free himself.

Clarence patted me on the back and commanded, "Get up, Robert!"

I followed the referee's instructions and lifted myself from Milton's chest.

I was standing near Clarence, waiting for him to announce me as the winner, when Milton suddenly sprung up from the ground, a gleaming white knuckle duster hooked to the fingers of his right hand.

Clarence used his presence of mind and stepped right in front of me.

Whoosh, I heard the knuckle duster move in the air and narrowly miss Clarence's jaw. I ran around the front of Milton and aimed mighty punches at his back in the style of my elder brother Victor.

He was thrown off balance and fell on his face on the red mud fighting ring. But he continued to retain in his fingers, the gleaming knuckle duster.

In a flash, Milton was up again, charging at me, taking a mighty swig at my jaw.

I ducked and went under him.

"Jai Hanuman," I yelled, the way Baloo had taught me.

The invocation worked and gave me the strength to lift Milton above my head, using his legs and hands as a fulcrum.

"Jai Hanuman," I shouted again.

Imagining that Milton was like the buckets of water that I lifted in the backyard of Hill Mansion, I continued to keep my opponent above my head.

Then I took a few steps forward and flung Milton away from me.

As he fell on his back with a loud thud, his gleaming knuckle duster slipped out of his grip and went rattling away, covered with red mud.

I rushed towards him, waiting for him to rise. But the impact of his fall to the ground seemed to have immobilised him.

He lay on the ground looking stunned and listless.

The referee ran towards us and began counting up to ten again.

Milton made no effort to rise.

"Robert is the winner of this friendly fight," Clarence announced.

He offered Milton his hand to help him up from the ground. Milton first sat up and then raised himself slowly from the ground, holding Clarence's hand.

Clarence pulled me next to him, took my hand and placed it in Milton's limp hand. As we shook hands silently, red mud mingled with sweat from Milton's hands rubbed into my palm.

Dattya, Anand and Baloo began beating their dholaks with wild abandon. Gangu Aai whistled in tune.

Victor came hopping into the ring, hugged me and raised me high above his head, using the back of my thighs as a lever.

As soon as Victor put me down, Dattya Dada placed his dholak aside on the ground, hoisted me by the legs, ducked and placed me on his strong, muscular shoulders. Anand and Baloo were beating their dholaks to celebrate my victory and Gangu Aai whistled to the beat ceaselessly.

However, in the celebration and the wild cheers from the audience, I seemed to have missed the angel for whose honour I had fought and defeated Milton Aguiar.

For, when Dada put me down after dancing with me on his shoulders for a few minutes, Rachael and her siblings weren't around.

I left the fighting venue and ran into our village's bylanes, knocking at the door of her house.

She opened the door and said angrily, "Choose man, choose, between me and your friends, the sons of the village servant lady."

I stood stunned, looking at her, without speaking.

She glared at me with her angry grey eyes. Her pretty face was twisted into a scowl. Her rose-petal, soft lips that I had dreamt of kissing for the rest of my life, contorted into a snarl, as she banged the door shut on my face.

I swear to uplift
my extended family

Rachael had given me what, at first, seemed like a difficult choice. But for me it was a choice that was easy to make. I had made up my mind, instantly. My brothers would never be sacrificed for her love, which anyway appeared so hollow and selfish now.

I might be sounding filmy and sentimental, but I wanted to prove that I was not a superficial hero, but a real one by standing by my extended family for the rest of my life. No girl, however pretty, could take my family away.

That night I had the soundest sleep of my life. I also woke up to the most pleasant dream of my life. Half a dozen pretty girls, all in short pink dresses, were smooching me endlessly, calling me hero and he-man, in chorus.

My shorts was soaked so much with the wet dream that I felt embarrassed to get out of my bunk. Luckily, it was vacation time and I could stay put in bed for some more time.

But the results – which would decide whether I went to the eleventh class or SSC that involved a board exam – were round the corner. My romance with Rachael, and the gruelling practice sessions for the challenge bout with Milton, had majorly chewed into my study time.

With my faith in God rapidly dwindling, I felt anchorless. There was no one in my peer group whom I could turn to for help to get me over this gnawing worry about my results.

The Bhoir family, were, of course, always there to unburden my problems. However, somewhere from the back of my mind, the thought kept creeping out that since they were all illiterate, they would not really understand the importance of passing the tenth standard and going to SSC. How wrong was I, indeed! For, it was Dattya Dada, accompanied by Anand and Baloo, who were the ones to disclose my results to me.

Soon after the ancient cuckoo clock chimed five times in the living room of Clarence's home in the evening on Tuesday, the 24th of May 1966, my three 'brothers' came looking for me in the balcony of his house that had also become my favourite haunt, second only to Hill Mansion, of course.

"You iz passing in all subjects and also standing thirty rank in class," Dattya announced, pushing open the small balcony door.

"Oh shucks!" I said, sounding more than a tad disappointed at rank thirty.

Dattya sensed my dissatisfaction and for a moment shut the box of my favourite pedas from Khandelwal Sweet shop that he was about to open in celebration of my results. Then he smiled knowingly, nodding his head, reopened the box and fed me with a peda.

"Don't be frighten…in the final board exam, you iz going to get the first class and getting to go good college," he declared.

Dada's prediction lifted up my spirits and I was really impressed that he after all knew about board exams, and that you needed a first class to get admission to a prestigious college. And I wondered how he had come to know about my results in the first place.

Even as I opened my mouth to speak, he said, "You wanting to ask, how I iz knowing all this, no?"

"Yes," I admitted.

"Your big brother Victor telling me all this and also asking to find you to tell you about your results," he said.

But it struck me that as Victor wouldn't have gone to Hill Mansion, my three brothers must have been the ones to have taken the initiative to find out about my results. Yes, my intuition was right, for Dattya confessed that Anand and Baloo had been keeping a watch for the village postman, hovering around White House. So when the postman delivered the letters that evening, Anand and Baloo accosted him and asked, if he had also given a letter in the name of Robert Pereira.

After the postman confirmed that, Anand and Baloo made a dash for Hill Mansion to inform Dada, who rushed to White House to find out about my results. Victor opened the door to my three brothers, who reflexively stepped back, expecting him to be cold to their intrusion.

But Victor grinned happily when he saw them and said, "Go and find your hero friend, the he-man and tell him he passed in all subjects and also got rank thirty in class."

"But thirty rank not good, no?" Dattya asked, anxiously.

"Don't worry Dattya, my brother will get a first class in the final board exam and go to a good college," Victor said.

As Dattya completed narrating how they learnt about my results, he remarked: "Your big brother is very nice and loves you lots. I am not knowing about board exams and first class and all that, but he iz nicely explaining for me." I couldn't disagree with Dada, because there seemed to be a sea change in Victor and the way he treated me these days. But I knew for sure that I loved Dattya Dada more than I loved my real brother Victor.

Dattya had, indeed, been the real elder brother. He had showered me with selfless love in my most difficult times, helping me to bust the tag of Ponga Pondya that had made my life so miserable all these years. I secretly swore before the altar of God at home that I would always be there for my extended family. I promised to return their love when I grew up into a man and earned money by setting up a carpentry business for them. And to fulfil the promise of uplifting my extended family, I decided to put in my best efforts for the eleventh standard board exams and secure a good college education to ensure that I got a well-paying job that would leave me with surplus money for my extended family.

Father Peter Coutinho
flattens my puff

On my first day in the eleventh standard, I sported my best puff in the style of my idol, the actor Dev Anand. Being fifteen years and nine months old, I didn't need Mummy's help in puffing my hair.

It was also the first time that I wore long pants to school, following St John The Evangelist's school principal Father (Dr) Alex Pimenta's permission that boys in the eleventh class could wear long pants, as he jokingly said, 'to hide their hairy legs'.

As I swaggered into class with my high, steady puff, dabbed with sparkling Brylcreem and my neat, well-pressed school uniform – grey trousers and white shirt – I noticed the girls turn their heads to look at me. But Sonam Malhotra, the most beautiful girl in class, perhaps, even the school, didn't look my way at all.

I joined my friend Jitu on the third bench in class.

Soon, our class teacher, Mr K. Murlidharan – with silver grey hair and a kind, smiling face – arrived. But he would only teach us essay writing, because the principal, who had a doctorate in English literature believed that he was the most qualified to teach English to eleventh standard students.

After Mr Murlidharan got to know his students in the first period of the day, since as class teacher he would be monitoring our overall progress, the principal Father Pimenta walked in for the second period, dressed in a spotless white cassock, a beaming smile lighting up his clean shaven face.

His cassock was so heavily starched that it seemed to stand stiff and alert like a soldier's steel armour. But the cassock appeared to be a wee bit short or maybe the starch made it look like that. In the case of other priests, you could barely make out their shoes as their flowing cassocks almost covered the footwear, but Father Pimenta's well-polished, gleaming shoes – with pointed fronts that was the style those days – were quite visible.

As I was on the third bench, I had a better view of him when he entered and I could see his long ears dance as he introduced himself, laughing aloud, like it was a funny thing to do.

"I am your English language teacher Dr Alex Pimenta," he said, breezily.

"Yes Father," we said together, happy that he didn't seem strict at all.

"Did you all say, 'Yes, Father'?" he asked, laughing heartily.

"Yes Father," we repeated in a long chorus to reassure him.

"No, no, no Father," he shouted over our chorus. "Stop it, at once!"

His jolly demeanour was replaced with an angry scowl. We were all shocked at this sudden anger and couldn't see the reason for it. Seeing us silent and scared, he laughed again, and said kindly, "Not your fault children; please let me explain."

He went to the big blackboard and wrote in big capital letters, right on top: DR ALEX PIMENTA. Turning around, he said: "My children, you will all call me Dr Alex, as I have a Ph.D. in literature and because I am nobody's Father or Daddy. Father is an address used by pious Catholics, whom I detest from the bottom of my heart. Doctor sounds better, right?"

"Right," many of us repeated. And we began explaining things to each other.

Since about forty students were talking at the same time, the class sounded noisy.

"Quiet!" shouted the principal, banging the duster hard on the table to make his point.

He rushed to the blackboard and wrote in all caps, again, "NOBODY BUT DR ALEX TALKS IN CLASS."

As he wrote each word with great force, his cassock kept riding over his stylish, high-heeled shoes, getting entangled in the tip of the boots. There was a roar of laughter all around the class, as Bashir Raza, the most mischievous boy in class, sitting on the bench behind me shouted fearlessly, "*Buddha* (old) Father is wearing Beatle boots!"

As the principal turned around, pirouetting on his boots, like a ballet dancer, the class fell silent instantly. He flung the chalk with which he was writing on the blackboard, aiming it at Bashir.

Chalk isn't really hard, but the speed and accuracy of the missile may have created some impact, for Bashir screamed, "Ahhhh!" The chalk hit Bashir's forehead and broke into a couple of pieces.

Now it was the principal's turn to laugh. And laughing he came towards Bashir. Holding Bashir's hand, the principal pulled him up from his seat, leading him towards his table, saying, "Come my boy, I want you to repeat what you said, standing in front of the class."

Bashir, who was very fair, turned extremely red in the face. His long ears that became redder than his face, seemed to be twitching. He stood in front of the class, pressing his chin into the tip of his chest, virtually hanging his head in shame.

"What's your name?" the principal asked Bashir.

"Bashir," he muttered.

"Be brave and give me your full name, Bashir," the principal said, laughing.

"Bashir Raza," he said, eating up his words as his jaw seemed to be trembling with fear.

"If your name is Bashir Raja, then you should behave like a king and not a rat," the principal said, laughing.

Bashir didn't seem to have the courage to correct his surname. To me it seemed that the principal had deliberately misheard the name.

"How old is your father, Bashir?" the principal asked.

"Fifty years," Bashir replied.

"I am forty-two years, my boy, and you have already made me old," the principal said. "I hope you treat your Daddy with some respect, since he is older than me."

"I'm sorry, Dr Alex," Bashir said, suddenly gathering his wits and even managing a smile.

"I have not really taken offence, Bashir Raza," the principal said, lingering over the surname to emphasise that he had got the name right.

Now Bashir grinned, his face shedding the red embarrassing tinge and his long ears looking cute, as they returned to their normal colour.

"Go back to your seat, Bashir," the principal said, patting him on his back.

"Thank you, Dr Alex," Bashir said.

The principal gripped Bashir's hand and shook it vigorously. "I like naughty boys, Bashir," he said, laughing. "But I like them more when they are braver."

Then Dr Alex, as we always addressed him thereafter, clapped his hands and asked the class to clap with him, saying, "Three cheers for Bashir Raza."

Dr Alex had great command over the English language, both spoken and written. As our class teacher would never tire of saying, "Dr Alex writes like an angel and speaks like a king."

But it was the Queen's English that Dr Alex was a stickler for. He seemed like a walking and talking encyclopaedia in English prose, poetry and grammar. The famous Bible of grammar, *Wren and Martin* seemed of no use to us when Dr Alex was around.

And he taught us with such tender love and care that English became the favourite subject of many of us in class. For students like Anwar Ali, Bashir Raza's thick friend, who were weak in English, Dr Alex had a unique solution. He asked Anwar to learn his prose, poetry and even grammar, singing the lesson to the tune of his favourite Hindi song. It worked. For, Anwar, who could never recite even the first two lines of a poem, used the movie *Junglee's* song '*Ehsaan tera hoga mujhpar*' to mug all the fourteen lines of W. H. Davies' famous poem, 'What is this life, if full of care, We have no time to stand and stare'.

Dr Alex even gave Anwar a big slab of Cadbury chocolate for the best recitation of the poem in class. The principal held a weekly class competition – one week for poetry recitation, then for prose, the third week for grammar and the fourth week competition was for essay writing, which he made the class teacher conduct. He seemed to have an unlimited stock of Cadbury chocolates. I had received two big Cadbury slabs as prizes for the best answers in prose and the best essay in the first two months itself.

Our only disappointment with our loving English teacher Dr Alex was that he never taught us any love poem, passing on the job to Mr Murlidharan. In fact, in the first month in class when Dr Alex came across Robert Burns' poem, 'My love is like a red, red rose', he skipped the page and said he would ask the great English poetry teacher Murlidharan to teach us "this beautiful ode".

"No, no, you are our English teacher," Bashir protested.

"Buddha Alex can't teach you love poems," Dr Alex said. "I am a celibate and know nothing about love." Then Dr Alex closed his eyes and seemed to be muttering a silent prayer. His face was serious and, I thought, I detected a trace of sadness in his expression.

Did he turn to the priesthood because of a broken heart, I wondered to myself.

But the silence and sadness soon disappeared and Dr Alex was back to his jolly self, grinning.

One day, he came up to me when class was over and whispered in my ears, "Did you see the latest Dev Anand movie *Jewel Thief*?"

"Yes," I said, shyly.

"I too saw it; the last show yesterday," he said so softly that only I heard him. "But don't tell anybody in class," he added, blushing, walking briskly out of class.

On Thursday, the 28th of September, 1966, Jitu and I were bunking the last two periods in class to be on time for the matinee show of Manoj Kumar's *Upkaar*. It was my sixteenth birthday treat to my friend. But, unfortunately, we bumped into Dr Alex standing outside the gate of the school. When we tried to retrace our steps and return to school, Dr Alex ran after us and holding us both, said, "Hey boys, go for your movie! I won't complain to your class teacher." We couldn't believe our ears, but Dr Alex held us by our hands and led us out of the school compound, saying, "Trust me boys; go enjoy."

But that was the last time we saw Dr Alex. For, the very next day when I arrived in school, Mr Murlidharan was there instead of the principal, saying he was taking the first English period.

"Why, sir?" we wanted to know.

Mr Murlidharan didn't seem the least offended that we preferred Dr Alex to him.

He smiled and said gently, "Friends, Dr Alex is slightly ill and is in hospital."

The class burst into tears. No matter how much Mr Murlidharan tried to console us, saying, "It's nothing serious," we wouldn't stop wailing.

Then when the Church bells rung loudly but slowly without a stop for a long time, a little after noon, we somehow guessed that Dr Alex was no more.

Mr Murlidharan came into class in the midst of the tolling, shaking like a reed and wailing like an infant.

"Dr Alex died of a massive heart attack," he said, bursting into tears.

He kept hugging us and we all took turns in trying to console him and wiping his tears. But no matter how much we tried, the sorrow just wouldn't go away.

That was Dr Alex!

The jolliest man in the world had kept his heart ailment a secret from all of us in school.

However, life goes on, and Dr Alex's successor Father Peter Coutinho walked into our lives.

A couple of shades fairer than Bashir Raza, the fairest person that I knew in our immediate circle, Father Coutinho had striking sky blue eyes and was a towering, domineering person.

As soon as we saw him, we realised that there was a striking contrast between him and Dr Alex. While our late dear principal laughed at the smallest things and at himself, Father Coutinho hardly ever smiled. Dr Alex was short and rotund. Father Coutinho was muscular and seemed as tall as a skyscraper in comparison to Dr Alex.

The manner of speech of the late and the present principal too differed. Dr Alex was clear in his speech and enunciated every word, while Father Coutinho ate up a lot of his words as he spoke, because he spoke with an almost shut mouth and words seemed to come hissing through his teeth.

Father Coutinho was a disciplinarian, who on the very first day in the school assembly made it clear that he didn't like naughty students and he was there to improve studies and ensure that students shone in the exams.

I remember Dr Alex once addressing the school assembly, when he said: "All work and no play makes Jack a dull boy. I want you all to enjoy your studies and I'd rather you fail than go mad cramming lessons that you don't understand. So study well, but study intelligently."

Dr Alex trusted his teachers and left them to conduct their classes independently. But Father Coutinho would pay surprise visits and barge into a class in the middle of a lesson and take an on-the-spot oral test on the subject that was being taught.

It was on one such surprise visit that he asked me to name India's first President during a social studies class. I knew who he was, but my memory failed me and I couldn't answer him, because Father Coutinho had been looking at me strangely, even before he asked the question.

The principal who was barely a month old by then came up to me and laughed. This was the first time we saw him laugh. But it was not a friendly, Dr-Alex-kind-of-laugh. It sounded rather mean and vicious to me. Then what Father Coutinho told me made me feel like punching his fair, tough, mocking face.

He said, "Roadside Romeo with the big puff of a small and cheap movie hero, stand up!"

I stood up but made no effort to hide my hurt and anger. Then he touched my puff, first gently, then roughly, with his right hand. I felt the blood rush to my face and my ears tingle. My classmates who had begun to murmur among themselves, turned silent. The only voice I could hear was that of Father Coutinho, hissing from clenched teeth, "Hero, huh."

Now he rubbed down my puff with both his hands and flattened it till my hair fell on my forehead like a fringe.

"Kneel down," he commanded. I didn't obey him.

"Kneel down, you cheap hero," he shouted, shoving me down with the force of his strong hands.

I knelt down, grinding my teeth with rage, looking up at him with anger and hatred as he was looking down at me and seemed to be suppressing a sinister laugh.

He suddenly turned his back to me and walked out of class. I got up from my kneeling position as soon as he had gone. Taking out from the back pocket of my trouser a comb, I straightened my dishevelled hair. I rubbed my front hair vigorously to stiffen it, so that the puff came up when I combed it in deft, upward circular motions.

"You look first class," my friend Jitu said, shaking my hand.

The social studies teacher Mr Satish Shetye walked to our desk and patted me on my shoulder, saying: "You look like my hero Dev Anand and I am proud of you."

"No sir, not just Dev Anand, he also looks like the greatest rock star Elvis Presley," Bashir Raza chipped in. I turned around to see my classmates, as I heard spontaneous cries of "Yay" all around.

"Thank you, sir," I replied, smiling.

When the school bell rang in rapid succession announcing the end of the day, I was touched to see my classmates surround me, shaking my hands vigorously, to show their sympathy, even admiration for me.

Father Coutinho's flattening of my puff was a blessing in disguise, because it won me so many more friends and admirers in class.

The best bonus was that the girls looked at me with open affection as they shook my hand. It was the first time in my life that I had held the hands of so many girls – exactly 17 of them if I remember right.

The only girl who didn't shake hands with me was Sonam. But she stopped by my desk and smiled, sending me almost into ecstasy. Oh! Thank God for blessing girls with such nice, soft hands and lovely smiles.

At the end of that memorable day, I went to sleep, smiling and saying to myself, "Lucky me."

Luck sprouts on me

Yes, lucky me! Father Coutinho's mean act of flattening my puff brought in loads of good luck and made my dreams come true. Against the principal's taunt of 'cheap hero', I was crowned 'real hero' by Sonam Malhotra, the most beautiful girl in class, who had ignored me in the tenth standard and continued to spurn efforts I made to chat with her in the final year in school so far.

A rare combination of modern and classic features, Sonam looked like either a queen or a goddess. It was difficult for me to make up my mind about the better tribute to her beauty.

We boys were all secretly in love with her. Some of us compared her to Madhubala, for her classic features and others to Saira Banu because of her modern looks. On days that she simply combed back her long golden brown hair with a central parting, she looked like Madhubala – the Indian film industry's most classic beauty. This made the Madhubala camp ecstatic.

Then on some days, she would puff her hair into a big, neat bun with exquisite strands of hair falling over her forehead like Saira Banu in her movies. And the Saira Banu clique would celebrate her beauty.

When I saw the Dev Anand-Saira Banu movie *Pyar Mohabbat* in the tenth standard, I had gone up to Sonam and told her that she looked exactly like Saira.

She had then rebuffed me with three harsh words, "Shut up, loafer!"

But the day after my puff was flattened, she came up to my desk in the morning before the class teacher arrived, smiling more widely than the previous evening, and said softly, "You are a real hero." I couldn't believe my ears, but I somehow knew that my good luck was growing.

Later, I stole a glance at her, seated on the last bench in the same row as me. She caught me in the act, but instead of ignoring me like in the past, she was smiling at me. I belonged to the Saira Banu camp, but now I was dreaming of quitting the camp of silent admirers and instead pictured myself holding her hand, not for a brief handshake but a long time.

That seemed so close…because after school ended that day, when I waited for her to pack her bag and walk down towards my desk, she smiled like an angel — walking gracefully in her neat, stylish shoes, unlike the rustic Rachael, who strode around barefoot, with jerky movements, throwing up dust in our village Golvada.

I don't want to sound cruel and heartless, but as I saw the smiling Sonam go by, I couldn't help comparing Rachael and her. For want of an original English expression, I am borrowing a popular Hindi saying and translating it – 'The difference between Sonam and Rachael was like that between the sky and the ground' – *zameen-asmaan ka fark!*

I fell so madly in love with Sonam that I was willing to pluck the stars for her and kiss the ground that she walked on. I believed that in Sonam I had found the right girl to spend my life with.

So each day after class, I would wait patiently for Sonam to pack her school bag, pass me on the third bench, smile and walk away gracefully like a goddess. Nearly a month after this ritual, one day I got a bit smarter and packed my bag quickly, waiting for her to pass by. As usual she smiled and walked away daintily. I took a deep breath and began strolling a few steps behind her. It seemed that she hadn't noticed me, for she didn't look back. As she reached the school exit gate, I quickened my pace to catch up with her.

Just then, I heard the loud, incessant ring of a bicycle. Seated on a brand new Raleigh bicycle was its proud handsome owner with dirty white shorts, an equally filthy white shirt and frayed plastic white sandals.

"Aay Robert, I am coming to taking you home on my *chuk-ahh-chuk* (shining) cycle", my 'brother' Anand shouted.

Sonam turned around and looked at me, barely a few feet behind her. She smiled. I thought her smile was so divine, much, much better than even a goddess.

"Hi Robert," she said, stopping her graceful walk.

She was waiting for me, smiling more than ever. I felt like a bird with wings and virtually flew to her in barely a second, almost knocking off the heavy school bag from my shoulder.

I walked silently beside her. There were so many nice loving things I wanted to tell her. But I was stuck for words. As we walked, she kept turning towards me and smiling. I smiled back, but kept mum. Then when she broke the silence, I concluded that she had the sweetest voice in the universe.

"Buddhu, why did you take nearly a month to walk home with me after school?" she asked.

"I, I..." I was stammering, trying to find a suitable answer.

"You are my real hero; so be like one and don't be shy," she said, smiling divinely again.

I was on cloud nine.

But Sonam brought me down to earth when she asked, "Who was that dirty looking boy on a brand new bicycle, offering to ride you home?"

"Who...whoo..." I stammered again. But this time I was not stammering, because I was in awe of her beauty.

I was stammering because I was disturbed…really disturbed when I realised that as I was drawn like a magnet to Sonam, I hadn't even bothered to respond to Anand's invitation to take me home on the Bhoir family's brand new bicycle. My extended family had been talking for a long time that they were saving money out of their earnings from carpentry to buy a 'dream cycle'.

I stopped walking and looked behind, further down the road. I spotted in the distance a few hundred metres away at the school exit, Anand still seated on his bicycle. I couldn't possibly see the expression on his face, but I was sure he must be very hurt.

My first impulse was to leave Sonam and run towards Anand, with the wings that Angel Papa had gifted to my legs and the resilience that Dattya Dada, assisted by my 'brothers' Anand and Baloo, had built into it.

But in a split second, I perished the thought and was telling Sonam, "Oh, that dirty boy lives some distance from my house in a hut."

"Really, in a hut?" Sonam asked, sounding slightly surprised.

"Hill Mansion," I said, quietly wiping a tear from my left eye.

"What's Hill Mansion?" she asked, her voice full of curiosity.

I felt the urge to tell her the story of my life, about my real family and my extended family…how my extended family were the ones who had made me a real hero, because they made me strong and inspired me with courage to live and fight.

But I didn't tell her anything, because that would shatter her image of me. If she heard my true story, I was scared that she wouldn't consider me a 'real hero' anymore. And I would lose her. I knew it was a mean and selfish thing to do, but I made up my mind that I would never mention Anand, Baloo, Dattya Dada and Gangu Aai to Sonam.

Shouldn't a 'real hero' be helping the poor, uneducated and underprivileged? But here I was, the one who was helped by the poor

Bhoir family. My image of a 'real hero' was a myth – so fragile that it could break into tiny bits any time.

I had grown physically strong enough to 'paste' any goon or bully, but I was too weak – emotionally and morally – to tell Sonam the truth about my childhood and my extended family. I had sacrificed Rachael for the Bhoirs. That was very brave of me. But then Rachael was like the ground. And Sonam was like the sky.

To reach for the sky and be there on cloud nine, I had to ignore the Bhoirs and their Hill Mansion – mine too, since I was the one to choose the name.

Sonam and I parted ways, as she entered the Reliable Mills residential complex, on the outskirts of our village Golvada. Her father was general manager at the mills.

As soon as I reached my home, White House, my first thought was to rush to Hill Mansion, and explain to Anand how and why I had forgotten him and his offer to ride me home on his new bicycle.

But then, I changed my mind.

I used to rush to Hill Mansion whenever I was in trouble or I needed help. Now, I was neither in trouble nor did I need help. In fact, I was loaded with luck, because I had walked the two-kilometre distance with Sonam, enjoying her beautiful company, listening to her lovely voice, floating on cloud nine. The explanation to Anand could wait, because it would spoil all the fun. I was sure that he would understand and forgive me *whenever* I did meet him.

Whenever!

Our late loving Dr Alex hated the word 'whenever' from the bottom of his heart, because it was such an indefinite word, giving no commitment. He was right, for I kept on putting off my visit to Hill Mansion day after day!

Anand and Baloo had been looking forward to taking turns in riding me down home from school on their bicycle. They had even talked about adding a carrier to the bicycle to accommodate my school bag that had really become heavy with my eleventh standard books. I too was mighty thrilled at the prospect and was waiting for their 'dream cycle' to arrive.

But after I was so shamelessly oblivious of Anand's presence on the very first day he came to ride me home, none of the two brothers showed up outside school again. That didn't distress me at all. I was happy that they didn't come, because there was no one around to disturb my blissful walk with Sonam.

In my bliss, I didn't even feel the weight of two heavy school bags, for quite often, I volunteered to carry Sonam's school bag for her. I loved to be so chivalrous, because her smile would then become more divine and in her pretty brown eyes, I could see a *diviner*…a soothsayer or a person who predicts future events; the future being us together forever.

Of course, my dream of holding her hand for an eternity didn't materialise, as we walked on a public road; and, unlike Rachael, I didn't kiss her, because I never met her outside of school, except for the walk home. Oh, yes! I did ask her to come out in the evening when we could meet some place or go to a movie. But she would retort, "Loafer, this is not possible. My father will kill me."

I had seen her once walk down the road with her father, who was more than six feet tall, muscular and with the thickest moustache I had ever seen. He had such thin, sharp lips that were shut so tight that they looked like a barber's razor.

I dared not look at him, though I stole a glance at her. She looked at me from the corner of one of her beautiful brown eyes, but didn't acknowledge my presence. But the next day when we were walking home, I couldn't stop myself from cracking a poor joke, saying, "Is your father general manager or an army general?"

I was surprised when she wasn't angry at my joke, but instead bestowed on me her most divine smile and said, "Papa, in fact, was a colonel in the army and took premature retirement to be with the family and stay close to his growing daughter, his only child."

Only child! She hadn't told me this all this while and I hadn't asked, because I was more interested in her than her family. But now I wanted to know more about her, because the time would soon come when I would need to visit her family, I thought.

"And your mummy, how is she? Strict?" I asked.

"Mummy passed away; that's why Papa left the army," she said. "I was so upset that I even lost a year and failed in the ninth standard." Her failing a year was another part of her life that I didn't know about.

"You know Robert, I am already seventeen years old and may be a year older to you," she said, looking very sad. I had never seen her sad, because she was always smiling at me. So my heart broke and I felt like it was split into thousands of pieces.

Balancing both our bags on each of my shoulders, I gently held both her hands.

I was not on cloud nine. But I felt so much of love for her, as a small tear drop trickled out of her right eye.

"Sonam, let me pass my board exams, then I'll come and meet your father and ask him…," she released her hands from me and put her right hand on my lips.

"Robert, don't be in such a hurry. We still have time and don't you want to complete your graduation before thinking of anything?" she said, blessing me again with her beatific smile.

That smile had rekindled my faith in God. I would pray every night, kneeling in front of the altar at home, begging God to never let us separate. I also asked God to forgive me for not going to meet the Bhoirs, whom I had all these years considered even closer than my real family.

Of course, I gave God a nice excuse for not visiting my loving extended family, because I now hardly stepped out of home after school and spent a lot of time studying for my board exams. But I did pray hard to God that He should help them get lots of work so that they could make enough of money to move out of Hill Mansion and own a real house.

Yes, there was one promise that I was breaking, which quite conveniently slipped my mind. I didn't even mention it in my prayers to God. I was supposed to help the Bhoirs set up a big carpentry business. What happened to that promise? Each time the promise crossed my mind, I had to quickly bury it, because it meant confiding in Sonam about the Bhoirs and the make-believe Hill Mansion that I had made them think all these years their hut was.

I seemed to have forgotten Anand, Baloo, Dattya Dada and Gangu Aai. But they hadn't. For, when I scraped through a first class, scoring 424/700 marks that would make me eligible for admission on a Christian quota to one of Bombay's best colleges, St Xavier's College, the Bhoir family went around Golvada, beating their dholaks and distributing boxes of pedas to all the thirty houses in the village. The Bhoirs had apparently bought the peda boxes from the earnings of their tiny carpentry business. My so-called 'bully' elder brother Victor proudly accompanied them.

When led by Victor, the residents of Hill Mansion came to our home, White House, with a pile of peda boxes, beating their dholaks with Gangu Aai whistling in tune, I burst into tears. I went close to them as I felt the impulse to hug all the four Bhoirs, one by one…but I didn't.

Shattered dreams,
Broken promises

❦

I didn't get my dream girl Sonam Malhotra as her father got her married to a fair, tall, handsome and rich business guy from her own community, soon after she appeared for her eleventh standard board exams. At least she was brave enough to find my home; and come with her wedding card, crying and pleading that she couldn't disobey her father as he wouldn't allow her to marry a Catholic boy.

I was no Prithviraj Chauhan to ride on a horse with shining armour and a gleaming sword and abduct her. So, the fragile hero that I was, I tamely gave in, though I declared that I would 'love her for a hundred years'.

She hugged me and cried for a long time. But my love for her didn't seem real, for I soon forgot her, busy as I got with Shirin, Pretti, Katy, Ernie, Jacinta, Priscila, et al in St Xavier's College, Bombay.

Priscila D'Sa became my favourite and most convenient girl friend, because she too lived in Thana, about a kilometer off Golvada in a village called Khatarwadi.

Unlike the people in Golvada, who retained the customs and traditions of their Hindu ancestors, Khatarwadi residents were westernised and unabashedly bragged that they had Portuguese blood running in their veins.

That perhaps was not far from the truth, because Priscila had light brown eyes, a peach complexion, and golden brown hair that was even a shade lighter than Sonam. It was a pity that she had a bob cut, but the neat and lovely fringe made her look so very attractive, as she carried her tall, regal frame with the poise of a princess.

I fell for her, because she was a close match to Sonam in beauty; and although she didn't have the classic features of Madhubala or the ravishing modernity of Saira Banu, she reminded me of Audrey Herpburn in the movie *Roman Holiday*.

But when it came to being snooty and snobbish, Priscila was notches above Sonam. She kept boasting about her fleet of full time servants, including a cook, who made 'the best dishes in the world', a house cleaner who kept her home 'spick and span' and a personal maid who was 'always at hand to attend to her'.

Compared to her aristocracy, we seemed so proletariat, with only one woman to do the cleaning. Mummy not only cooked but also washed our clothes. Priscila's snobbery didn't bother me, because she made me feel on top of the world and often greeted me with the words, "Hi Handsome Macho." I responded by always addressing her as "Beautiful Princess".

In less than two months after we joined college in July 1967, Priscila and I came to be labelled as a 'couple' in college.

She was studying for a B.Sc degree and I for a B.A. degree, but as we got closer, we would wait for each other after college and travel home together for an hour in the local train from Victoria Terminus to Thana.

Then we would walk the forty-five-minute long four-kilometre distance to home together. While she took the diversion to Khatarwadi at Utalsar naka, I would walk at a tangent towards my home in Golvada.

On my seventeenth birthday on Thursday, the 28th of September, 1967, Priscila gave me a royal treat, which began with a nice, long smooch in a cosy corner of the college soon after classes were over, followed by a sumptuous lunch at an expensive restaurant. The grand finale of the treat was a regal four-rupee ride in a tonga from Thana station to Golvada village, instead of our arduous walk home.

Then as we dismounted from the horse carriage, there was a surprise in store. She fished out of her handbag, a sleek looking silver bracelet with my name engraved on it. We began walking from near the cross, where the tonga halted, towards my home, White House, as I was going to introduce Priscila to my family.

As we entered the lane to my home, I spotted Anand, Baloo and Dattya Dada, standing quietly, several feet away from the gate of White House. Dada – I just couldn't drop that tag from his name – held a box of sweets, which I could figure out even from the distance was my favourite pedas from Khandelwal Sweet shop.

The three brothers – my extended family not-so-long-ago – looked at me, silently. They seemed unsure what to do…should they smile, laugh, come to me and wish me happy birthday, and hug me? Four years ago on the same day, my thirteenth birthday, they had hosted for me a big birthday bash at their home, Hill Mansion.

More than a party of merry making, it was an occasion to celebrate my transformation from a soft weakling to a strong boy.

Today, the brothers, who had taught me how to live and fight, seemed to be waiting for me, patiently, silently – not knowing how I would react to their presence.

They were not asking me to keep my promise of building their carpentry business, which I had made to no one but myself. But what would I lose if I, at least, smiled at them, if not hug them.

I turned towards Priscila, who had noticed them standing and looking in my direction. She smiled at them…a nice, sweet smile. Then she was beckoning them to come along.

"Poor things, they seem so afraid to approach you, handsome macho," she said.

Dada walked towards me, while Anand and Baloo continued standing. Dattya Dada, my hero – not-so-long-ago – handed the peda box to me and said, "Happy Birthday…." He swallowed the rest of the words. I detected a tear forming in his eye, but he quickly flicked it away, like it were a dust particle.

Dada wasn't smiling at all, and I noticed that his hair was not long anymore, but closely cropped. Then Dada turned his back to me and walked away. Anand and Baloo followed him, without turning to look at me.

I felt the urge to rush towards the departing brothers, stop them and hug them for dear life. Priscila was tugging at my arm, asking excitedly, "Who were those guys, former servants or what?"

Dada, whose ears were always pricked up, alert as he was to wild foxes outside Hill Mansion, seemed to have heard Priscila's query; for, though he was some feet away, he turned around and grinned, waving at me. My Dada was a sportsman after all, and took Priscila's remark really sportingly.

Anand and Baloo too turned around and were grinning, waving breezily at me. I don't know if I was imagining but I thought I could see the smallpock marks dance with glee on Baloo's face. I waved back.

Then I took a step forward, ready to sprint towards them.

Get set, ready….

I stopped at go.

The distance made me stop. It was not the distance between me and the Bhoir brothers, as they were just some feet away from the cross and I could have reached them in a few seconds.

It was the distance that I had built in my heart, between me and them that kept me from running and hugging them…only my heart, for I was sure that their hearts were still pure and full of unconditional love.

My heart looked at the conditions, the circumstances and whether my girlfriend would continue to call me those good names if she found out who the Bhoirs really were.

I had been sure that Sonam wouldn't have continued calling me 'real hero' if she discovered that the Bhoir brothers were the ones who made me one.

And Priscila, would she continue calling me 'handsome macho' if I told her that the credit, at least for the macho part went to the guys whom she thought were my former servants.

Nah, never, she would have exclaimed, using one of her pet phrases to express her disapproval and thrown me out like a rotten apple.

Then as I held Priscila's hand and knocked on the entrance door of White House, I quietly wiped a tear trickling down my eye.

Epilogue

Today, forty-eight years later, when my family is not around, I still shed tears when I think of Hill Mansion, where lived my loving extended family, the Bhoir brothers.

My extended family seems like a dark secret that I have hidden from all those close to me – the family that I was born into, my girlfriends, and now my wife and children.

Why have I done this? Why haven't I openly acknowledged the role of those who taught me how to rise from sorrow and weakness; to live and fight; how to become strong.

The more I think about how the poor but strong residents of Hill Mansion gave me their only possessions – courage and unconditional love – while I gave them nothing in return, the sadder I feel…and tears keep pouring down my eyes.

But what is the use of my tears? It won't heal the hurt and the stab of betrayal.

I can see them clearly even now…waiting for me to hug them, first when I passed my eleventh board exams and then on my seventeenth birthday, just like I used to when I needed them, in and outside Hill Mansion. That would have sealed our bond and healed the pain that I had caused to them by becoming an alien, though they were more than real family.

The more I think about those days, the more I cry.

Crocodile tears, really!

Crocodile tears…I shouldn't be using the phrase, because Dr Alex hated it from the bottom of his heart, as he believed it was one of the worst clichés he had ever come across.

"Fake tears sounds shorter and forceful," Dr Alex would say.

But personally, I prefer 'crocodile', because 'fake' reminds me of the fake person – both friend and brother – that I had proved to be. Crocodile may remind me of a monster, but at least that creature doesn't seem so bad in comparison to a fake person.

Anand, Baloo, Dattya Dada and Gangu Aai are not around to console me with their pure, selfless love. To tell you the truth, I don't know where they really are. I have never bothered to search for them.

After my graduation, I did a post-graduation in management and then worked on various jobs in different metros in the country, mostly away from my home town Thana. In my hectic life, the Bhoir brothers were a forgotten memory.

When I visited home in the late nineties, after working abroad for many years, I returned to Golvada village to find that its environs, once a rustic place, had acquired the look of an urban landscape with tall skyscrapers dotting the area.

Hill Mansion too had gone, swallowed up by hawkish builders. The woods around were hacked and in its place were tall, grey buildings. I had then not bothered to find out where the Bhoir brothers were.

When I recently visited the place out of sheer curiosity, I saw around the area where Hill Mansion used to be, a multi-storeyed building 'Hill Towers' as the builders had maintained the elevated position of the place to give the building an aesthetic and royal feeling.

For a fleeting moment I thought about the love that I had shared with the folks in Hill Mansion. For a split second, I even imagined that they were around.

But, even if the residents of the demolished Hill Mansion were around, would I still love them?

I deeply doubt it.

Because I have moved on…to bigger things and greener pastures.

After I had refused to acknowledge them on two occasions, I would occasionally bump into the Bhoir brothers in Golvada. While they shouted a loud 'hello, how iz you, brother', I would reply with a mere nod.

My childhood friends and hero – my once extended family – had become mere nodding acquaintances. I had outgrown them and we seemed to be from two different worlds.

The crocodile tears are coming again. But crocodile tears are not real. So, it doesn't really hurt…because I have ultimately turned out to be like many of my kind…shallow, though successful.

Recommended Reading

Life is What You Make It

Preeti Shenoy

"A simple narration with umpteen smart phrases makes the book a one session reading." – The Times of India.

"This book promises to be a show stealer." – Deccan Chronicle

What would you do if destiny twisted the road you took?

What if it threw you to a place you did not want to go?

Would you fight, would you run or would you accept?

Set across two cities in India in the early eighties, this book is a gripping account of Ankita Sharma's life, who has the world at her feet. She is young, good-looking, smart and has tons of friends and boys swooning over her. But six months of being in a premier MBA college, she is a patient in a mental health hospital.

How did Ankita get here? What were the events that led to this? Will she ever get back her life?

It is a deeply moving and inspiring account of growing up, the power of faith and how determination and an indomitable spirit can overcome even what destiny throws at you.

Preeti Shenoy is an author and an artist based in Bangalore, India. She also specializes in pencil portraits and holds an internationally recognized qualification from UK in portraiture.

ISBN: 978-93-80349-30-5, Price: ₹ 120, Pages: 224, Binding: Paperback

Googled by God
Pulkit Ahuja

This is a fast moving financial thriller that takes the reader on a journey to the dark realms of entrepreneurship and technology. Revolving around the ever changing worlds of stock markets, investments and money, the reader soon finds himself in the middle of a dangerous game of emotions and karma.

Pulkit Ahuja is a serial entrepreneur with experience in founding and running disruptive technology start-ups in education, ad-tech and transportation domains. He is an MBA Gold Medallist in Finance, formerly associated with Standard and Poor's Capital IQ.

ISBN: 978-93-82665-44-1, Price: ₹ 195, Pages: 178, Binding: Paperback

Ready..Steady..Exit
P.C. Balasubramanian

Gautam completed CA after several attempts and to his luck, landed up with Anand, a close friend and brilliant CA, to launch an Accounting Services company named FAB. When Vimal comes in with a delectable package, an impressive consulting profile and his smart and very beautiful sister Ruchi, FAB grows… but relationships deplete.

This book is a humorous, dramatic, romantic, enlightening and entertaining read.

P.C. Balasubramanian (PC to some and Bala to others) is a Chartered Accountant by qualification and an author by accident. He is one of the promoters and directors of Matrix Business Services India P Ltd, and has to his credit two bestsellers.

ISBN: 978-93-82665-40-3, Price: ₹ 120, Pages: 184, Binding: Paperback

It Doesn't Hurt to be Nice

Amisha Sethi

This is Kiara's story and the wisdom she achieves through the various dramatic and hilarious experiences, as much as it is yours. *You* are the 'hero' of the book, who can beat the most stubborn of villains...our fear, unkindness, selfish interests, negative thoughts and jealousy. *You* are the 'heroine' who is sharp and witty in talking, selfless and caring in love, and charming and beautiful inside out, like none other (perhaps a 2.0 version of you).

Amisha Sethi is an executive scholar from Kellogg School of Management, Northwestern University, Chicago, and holds an MBA degree in Marketing from Amity Business School. She was awarded the "Young women rising star" at World Women Leadership Congress 2014.

ISBN: 978-93-82665-48-9, Price: ₹ 175, Pages: 144, Binding: Paperback

The Great War of Hind

Vaibhav Anand

Around 12000 B.C., Hindustan as we know it today (or Hind), comprised five kingdoms of man, sandwiched between Parbat – the kingdom of the Gods in the north, and Lunka – the kingdom of the demons in the south. The 'Legend of Ramm' unravels the story of the military general called Ramm in the kingdom of Ayodh and how his actions came to define our world as we know it today.

Vaibhav is a marketing professional working with an MNC by day, blogger/ writer/ poet by night. Author of the bestselling If God Went to B-School, Vaibhav is also one of the top contributors to Faking News, the satire portal.

ISBN: 978-93-82665-46-5, Price: ₹ 175, Pages: 184, Binding: Paperback